EYEHEART EVERYTHING

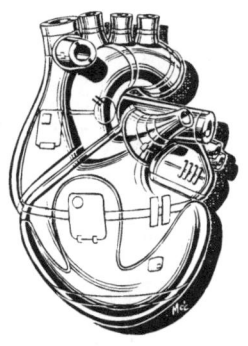

EYEHEART
Volume 5, Number 5, Issue 30

Published by Mykle Systems Labs
5536 NE 27th Ave, Portland, Oregon, 97211
www.mykle.com/msl

A division of Time-Life-Warner-Turner,
a subdivision of Sony-Sony-Sony,
in partnership with Beatrice,
The Trilateral Commission,
and The Gnomes Of Zurich.

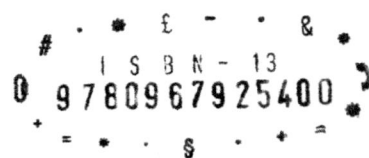

0 1 1 2 3 5 8 13 21 34 55

Second Edition: Hopefully Before Christmas, The Year 2010
Additional second-edition material copyright © 2010 Mykle Hansen
First edition copyright © 1999 Mykle Hansen   mykle@mykle.com
All Rights Reserved

"Slowly, Languorously" first appeared online in Clean Sheets (www.cleansheets.com). The author is
grateful for the nine dollars. "Homosexuals In The Military," "Vote Bozo," "Letters To The
Manufacturers of Alley Katz Katz Food," "Poor Ivan Is In Love," "The Great Mechanico," "The
Talking Bottle Of Gin" and "Need More Energy!" first appeared in previous issues of EYEHEART
and are Copyright © 1996, 1995, 1994, 1993 and at various other times throughout history.

Illustrations on pages 13, 57, 77, 95, 136 by Ed Statsny.
Illustration on page 51 by Kevin Kirkbride.
Book and cover design by 6rady "6rady made this" Clark.

The author would like to thank the Smith-Corona Company, makers of fine typewriters, and the
staff of Ace Typewriter & Equipment Company in Portland, saviors of same.

WELCOME TO THE SOPHISTICATED WORLD OF DISCRIMINATING PEOPLE WHO
LOVE THE FEELING OF WEARING FINE, SUPPLE LEATHERS, SILKY SUEDES AND
LUXURY SHEARLINGS. THIS GARMENT IS A NATURAL DELICATE LEATHER. IT
SHOULD BE WORN CAREFULLY, SINCE ROUGH WEAR MAY EASILY DAMAGE THE
LEATHER. SUPPLENESS WILL INCREASE WITH USE. LEATHERS AND SUEDES,
BEING NATURAL PRODUCTS, SHOW ALL NATURAL MARKINGS. ALTHOUGH ALL
OUR SKINS HAVE BEEN CAREFULLY MATCHED, SLIGHT VARIATIONS IN COLOR
CANNOT BE AVOIDED. IN FACT, THIS IS YOUR ASSURANCE THAT THE GARMENT
IS MADE OF GENUINE SKINS. ALL GARMENTS MADE IN SUEDE SHED WHEN NEW.
A SLIGHT BRUSHING WILL REMOVE THE LOOSE NAP. THIS IS NOT A DEFECT, BUT
A CHARACTERISTIC OF FINE SUEDE. ALL LEATHER GARMENTS SHOULD BE
CLEANED BEFORE THEY BECOME TOO SOILED. USE A SOFT CLOTH DAMPENED
IN LUKEWARM WATER TO SPONGE OFF LIGHT SURFACE SOIL. SEND YOUR
GARMENT TO A RELIABLE SUEDE AND LEATHER CLEANER ONLY! ENJOY YOUR
GARMENT.

Congratulations! You have won a pony.

for GREGORY and GESINE

Contents

Here's a simple fact: The best stories are ones that speak right to you, that read like someone is talking to you. Humor is the same way. The best stuff talks to you, even if they ramble like a crazy person. Many humor writers lack this knowledge or gift. They often talk at you or lob their high-minded witticisms over your head.

Mykle Hansen is one of the good ones. He is your friend. He wants to make you laugh (about stuff like unfortunate UHF reception, Armenia, and weird dreams) and he wants to protect you (by telling you what big red buttons not to push and teaching you about mind control).

I was lucky enough to discover Hansen's humor through this book when I was taking over the small press section at Powell's way back in 1999. I appreciated the index of subject matter on the back and the impressive home printing and binding job. I thought to myself: this guy is really funny and ambitious! I gotta meet him. And I also gotta tell people about this book and sell a boatload of them.

So we met and became friends. We went to a laser light show together (Beastie Boys), did some readings together, and talked about boy stuff. I even borrowed money from him a few times.

One of the readings we did together was in the basement of a cafe on NE Alberta. It was called "Strip Poetry" and Mykle had created this roulette wheel with numbers on it. Before each person read, they had to spin the wheel and take off that many pieces of clothing. Everyone was wearing layer upon layer of clothing but I still ended up nearly naked. Just my boxers remained. I think Mykle was left wearing a sombrero, but I could be wrong. I have blocked it out probably.

I like Mykle because he does weird stuff like that. And since the release of Eyeheart Everything back in '99, he has just gotten weirder. I mean, where do I begin? The pseudo-religious advice column or the book about a man being eaten by a bear?

But to tell you the truth, this book is still my favorite. It's ridiculous, smart, and totally inventive. Open it up and let it start speaking to you, like a crazy naked person wearing a sombrero.

Kevin Sampsell
Fall 2010

Menu

There's ten small men on poles next to the Theater
Ideal, balancing on the ends of tall poles and upon
themselves balancing more poles, and at the tops of
those poles far overhead are precariously spinning
plates, and on those plates are today's special entrées.
Meanwhile, deep within the earth's crust, a team of
tunnel-boring engineers are directing the forward
movements of a modern tunnel-boring device, guided
by readings taken from the cerebral cortex of an
anaesthetized truffle-hunting laboratory pig, based on
our infrared satellite predictions of a huge subterranean
truffle network in the vicinity of St. Remy au Perdue.
Their work continues apace, and may supply our
second course. For our third course, staff acrobatic
skydiving barbequeuists are even now packing their
parachutes, preparing to rise 5000 meters above the
western aviary preserve and then to dive. Their
mission: to swoop silently down upon the high-altitude
quail that have been observed there, hand-capturing,
-executing, -cleaning, -seasoning, -stuffing and finally
lighting ablaze said quail in free-fall, encasing them
within special reinforced free-falling hibachii, before
finally deploying their 'chutes at the last possible
moment. It's a risky job. The reinforced hibachii,
upon re-entry, will be retrieved by gyrocopter and
rushed to our special reconstructive facility, where the
black-box recording devices will be analyzed for signs
of charring, seepage, or dryness. Of the perhaps
half-dozen retrieved candidates, only the finest will be
brought to your table as tonight's main course — the
others will be sealed within drums of fast-drying
cement, loaded aboard our submarine and propelled to

the center of the Indian Ocean, where we will perhaps lose track of them. Only the best for our patrons. As a contrast, our fourth dish consists of bowls of fine potting soil which have been seeded with exotic fruit pits. A spoon is provided for the impatient. After the fruit plate, coffee or crack cocaine will be served, and then a desert of a light pâté of the noses of small, helpless, extremely friendly and fun-loving animals who depend on their sense of smell for survival. 👁

Mary Beans and her Amazing
Personal Organizer

Mary Beans and her amazing personal organizer
cornered me at a work-party last week, the one held at
the Swollen Vole. She said that three months earlier,
on August 13th, I had "promised" to call her sometime
"soon" and that she had at that point taken me to
mean within that week, but had later extended that
definition of "soon" to encompass a thirty-day period,
in deference to my busy work schedule, and that upon
the exhaustion of the thirty-day period of expectation
she had decided that it would be wise to assume a final
all-encompassing definition, a definition of "soon" any
layman would consider clearly over-generous, of ninety
days, and she showed me all of these dates and periods
in her amazing personal organizer, and sure enough, it
was November 14th and the ninety day period had
elapsed by three more days. I told her I lost her
number, and she pointed out that she had taken the
twin precautions of both pinning a card with her home
number written on it to the wall of my cubicle on Day
Three of the ninety-day phone-watch, and also of
mailing to me at my home address (she is friends with
the Human Resources Lady and apparently has all the
data on me that can be had) a similar card. Plus, she
says, her number is listed in the telephone book under
Beans, Mary. I told her I was too drunk to explain,
and she turned to the page where she had been keeping
track of my behavior since I arrived at the Swollen
Vole. This was drawn as a time-line, extending left to
right, bisecting the small beige note-page, starting on
the left edge at 5:30pm, the official start-of-party.
Above the line were indicated her own actions: arrival,
5:45 (fashionably late). At 5:54, a Manhattan was

obtained, and this was finished at 6:01, after which there was a ten minute cooling-off period, during which time several other employees of our office arrived in a group. Screwdriver at 6:11, and my own arrival (indicated below the bisecting line) at 6:38 was two drinks after that, but, she showed me, I had had only one drink, what appeared to be a gin and tonic, at 6:39, and was clearly only half-way through drinking it at 6:41, the moment at which she approached me with her amazing personal organizer and began her remarkably well-documented tirade. I said that it appeared she was too drunk to listen to an explanation, and she asked me if I thought she was pretty, and I said sure she was, which was a lie, and she pointed out to me that she had asked me this same question, in order to confirm my position, no less than seven times in the course of day-to-day inter-employee fraternization. And I was certain that I had not told that uncomfortable lie seven whole times, but she had records, and what did I have besides my faulty memory? I began to try to tell her that she was acting strange, and was clearly distraught, and that it was maybe unfair of me not to have simply told her the truth: that I found her mousy, skinny, odd, that her way of looking at me made me want to leap out of my skin and run away, and that I was flattered in an abstract sense by her interests, whatever they were, I sort of assumed romantic-to-carnal, but that I was just a contractor, not interested in getting involved with my co-workers on this mangy three-month job. But of course I didn't get that far. Instead, Mary Beans first struck me across the jaw with her amazingly hefty

5

personal organizer, and then as I reeled back, demanded an appointment. A date, in other words, and she flipped through the pages sarcastically, poring through her upcoming social calendar. Evening of Monday the 21st? Open. Tuesday the 22nd? Open. Wednesday the 23rd there was an appointment to watch Ally McBeal, but that could be postponed. Thursday? Wide open! She waved the pages in my face.

My lip was split. I tasted blood with my next sip of gin and tonic. I held my glass to the light. There was a tiny red storm cloud slowly tumbling inside. I didn't know what to say. Honestly, I am at the mercy of people like Mary Beans, who have schedules and are organized, and who make it so difficult for me to tell them the truth. She demanded a piece of my time, to compensate for the crime she felt I had committed. I had simply hoped that I would fail to call her and she would get the message, but no, Mary Beans only accepts messages in the format that her personal organizer can digest. And I tried to tell her that I had a girlfriend already, which would have been a lie if I'd been able to get it out, and I didn't know any way to talk my way back to the truth from all the polite little lies she had wrung out of me so far.

So ... so Thursday at 6pm, a movie TBA, dinner, reserved unstructured time on into the evening thereafter. She wrote it down triumphantly in thick red felt pen, she made me sign it, and she tore out a meeting-reminder slip from the back of her little leatherette book and scribbled the appointment on it, wrote DON'T FORGET!!! and underlined it three times, then stuck it in my hand, squeezed that hand, and planted a little kiss on my cheek before turning towards the door and falling over halfway there.

Drunk people fall over in bars, certainly, and some of them hit their faces on small wooden tables as they fall, certainly, and some of those tables it must be said are unfortunately set with glasses and flatware, which those drunk people occasionally catch in the face. It's rare, but it happened, and a bunch of us rode along with her to the emergency room, where she smiled coyly at me as the blood streamed from her face, and when they came to take her in for X-rays and stitches, an orderly tried to take from her her amazing personal organizer, but she screamed, cursed and held onto it with all her might, because she knew she had me trapped inside. 👁

Return My Sweater Or Face Civil Action!

I will never again allow myself to be coated with oil,
suspended by my ankles and slapped with sides of beef
so that you may impress your thesis advisor with your
outsider credentials. I have had enough. I will not
shave, dye, pierce or tattoo myself, or any of my pets,
for you ever again. I will not cut any more holes in the
roof of your car. I will not resist arrest. I will not sit
through any more drunken screenings of Pink
Flamingos with your tittering, abrasive friends. I will
not pretend to be your former employer when your
future employer calls me at midnight, asking whether
you are "a hottie" or "just a bitch." Don't ask me to,
ever again.

You cannot store any more movie memorabilia at my
mother's house. You may not park your dead '68
Buick hearse, that leaks three kinds of fluids and rusts
obnoxiously, and smells of death, in my brother's
driveway. You may not borrow my car battery any
longer. I need it for my car. Please get your bicycle off
of my fire escape, and take your carpet remnants too.

Please, please, take home your vast, tumorous,
indolent, violent hairy cat. I cannot say what might
happen if you don't do this soon. I have stopped
feeding it, I warn you. I am not going to say anything
about the feelings I have for this animal, or what its
living here has cost me, in dollars and in turmoil. Just
take it — or else.

I have called all of your friends and told them what
you are like.

I have called all your friends and informed them of my decision to sever all ties with them. I am returning the bottle of Spike your mother sent after our Thanksgiving dinner — I never opened it. I never used the cologne you gave me, you can have that back as well. And I no longer have any use for that thing in the basement. I have told the super about you, and posted a picture of you in the foyer where the neighbors can see it. None of them will let you in.

I would like my sweater back. It's my favorite sweater. I told you so when you took it — which I never said you could do. I NEVER LENT YOU MY SWEATER. I was given that sweater by a dear friend who died of an ear infection in South America, Hector, I told you about him. But I doubt you care about me, or Hector, or Hector's sweater which has shrank two sizes since you've had it. It doesn't fit you any more, or me, but I want it back. That's all I'm asking.

I have consulted with an attorney, regarding said sweater, and he has assured me that I am entirely in the right, and should the issue eventually be aired in court, the law will back me up. But I don't want that, and I don't think you do either. Just mail it to me, in whatever condition you may find it, as soon as you read this, and there won't be any trouble. Enclosed is a self-addressed, stamped envelope. ❧

Homosexuals In The Military

It is reported in our files that tall people are less short than normal people. It is reported by our spies that tall people are statistically more deviant in this respect. It is reported in our files that normal people are in all ways more normal than abnormal people, and therefore better from a governmental standpoint, and more aesthetically pleasing to the Census Bureau. It is the policy of this organization to subvert contemporary ideas of normalcy, and to replace them with our own far more normal values.

The two organizations that stand in the way of homosexuals' relentless pursuit of human rights — at the cost of widespread public embarrassment! — are the United States Armed Forces and the Boy Scouts of America. Today the President issued a decree striking down the age-old ban on homosexuality in the Boy Scouts. Later today the newly formed Boy's Council On Those Nasty Homosexuals accused the president of subverting contemporary ideas of normalcy, with the intent to replace them with his own far more normal values.

The two organizations that stand in the way of the president's relentless pursuit of human rights for homosexuals — at the possible expense of a certain loss of innocence of every citizen above the age of thirty! — are the U. S. Congress and the Supreme Court. Today the Supreme Court struck down, by Presidential decree, the age-old ban on homosexuality in the Congress. It is reported in our files that more than ten percent of all members of Congress are homosexuals, or in some other way not normal. The freshly-gerrymandered House Unspeakable Activities Committee issued a statement today to the effect that allowing homosexuality in the Congress will present insurmountable morale problems. Spokesmen and spokespersons insisted that separate bathroom facilities will become necessary, at a cost to taxpayers of over three hundred million billion trillion dollars, at a time when the federal debt is so large that some members of Congress get all turned-on just thinking about it. It was also insinuated that the House of Representatives would have to be redesigned completely, to accommodate one long row of chairs, over four hundred seats wide, so that no Representative would have a homosexual sitting directly behind him.

Today a source from deep within the Boy Scouts of America confessed to the press that a homosexual Representative had indeed been sitting directly behind him, on and off for many months, and that he had actually kind of enjoyed it.

Today the press attacked the Senators and the Representatives for their dishonesty and their sycophantic devotion to normalcy. The press, armed with makeshift spears and explosive exposés, surrounded the Capitol building for twelve hours, cutting off all access other than interviews. One man, an Eyewitness Mobile News Unit driver, loaded his Eyewitness Mobile News Unit with plastic explosives and attempted a suicide assault on the blockades, with a seething mass of journalists behind him set to stream

in through the gaping hole. But his Eyewitness Mobile
News Unit Special Live Report was preempted by the
network affiliate's Super Double Special Live Instant
Action News Report of his kamikaze attempt, and the
cancellation took all the fight out of him. He turned
his videocam upon himself, thrust the lens in his
mouth and pulled the trigger. His epiglottis just
couldn't handle the fame. The National Guard
restored peace to the scene with tear gas and rubber
bullets.

Today the just-coalesced citizen's action group, Citizens
Who Are Afraid Of Homosexuals For Some Reason,
rallied around the Washington Monument in protest of
the President's war on normalcy. When the monument
swelled to six times its usual size, the protesters ran
away. A Navy team of combat urologists was sent in to
defuse the situation, and then the National Guard
restored peace to the scene with tear gas and rubber
bullets.

In our files are listed the names of all citizens in the
United States who are male, who are living with other
males other than family members, who have been
living together for more than a year, who are not
macho. This information is easily culled from mailing
lists. In a national security situation, these men can all
be rounded up in the middle of the night and sent to
detainment camps in the Arizona desert which are
already constructed. In our files are listed the names of
all citizens of the United States who have purchased
AIDS-therapeutic drugs such as ATZ. Beleaguered

pharmaceutical companies are happy to supply us this information. In a national security situation, these citizens could all be rounded up in the middle of the night and made to just disappear, forever. In our files are the names of all citizens of the United States who exhibit a standard Normalcy Fluctuation Index greater than thirteen per cent, calculated on their answers to the previous U.S. Census. In a national security situation, these citizens could be targeted by orbiting satellites as soon as they left their houses in the morning.

None of this will be possible if homosexuals are allowed to join the military. 👁

Slowly, Languorously

Slowly, languorously you roll your pink socks up your smooth calves as I slip one leg, then two, deeper into the legs of my loose, loose trousers. You slide seductively farther away on the tan print sofa, shuddering slightly as you do the clasp on your brassiere, slide into your dress, your boots, your galoshes. My cock grows soft, softer as you spray me with the cold, wet garden hose. I talk about the economy to get you even less excited, and then I don my moist, dripping poncho.

I move even further away, humming lowly as I file my change of address forms. (The way you stop calling me makes me so steamy.) Now you are shaving your head, piercing your nose, changing your name, moving to Austria. You don another sweater. My cock is so flaccid and squeezably soft that I grow incontinent. Your nipples droop with restrained boredom. An icicle dangles seductively from your crotch.

"Are you ready?" I telegram as I mount my turgid space probe, clamping down my helmet and my thick, thick gauntlets. "I am pushing, ramming myself farther away. Beg me to leave!"

"Oh, god yes, go away, oh!" is your e-mail response from your concrete bunker. There you have encased yourself in quick-drying plaster and dry leather straps. The buckles chafe. My manhood shrinks to the subatomic scale. Your tits fall off. The rocket fires. I exit you.

"Oooh! Yeah! Farther! FARTHER!" you scream as I approach infinity. My joints stiffen. "Hold on ... I'm going!"

"Me too! I'm going! I'm gone!"

◉   ◉   ◉

The universe fades as we anticlimax together. I roll off the sofa and look for a cigarette but the cigarettes are all smoked. Then I remember we're both dead anyway, so I smoke myself. ◈

Vote Bozo

A pollster called me up to ask me who I planned to vote for. I told her I planned to vote for the candidate with the big floppy hat. She went on to inform me that the other candidate also has a big floppy hat, bigger and floppier, even, and that my candidate's hat is rumored by scientists to actually be quite stiff. I told her I wasn't listening and she said her candidate doesn't listen either. I asked her who she worked for. She said she was from Citizens to Change My Mind.

I told her: I'm sticking with my candidate. Not only does he have a floppy hat and big goofy shoes, he'd had a real red rubber nose, American made, ever since he was mayor of Palm Springs. He sleeps with it on, though his wife protests. I told her: I demand real frivolity in government. I demand a Bozo.

She told me she liked that in a man, one thing led to another and soon enough we'd arranged a lunch date at a cheap eatery near my flat, a trendy place known for its vox populi, usually on rye. I waited there for her in my bleeding-heart-red jacket and size 24 shoes. When she arrived I was startled by her unconservative looks. Her hair: curly red. Her eyes: cobalt yellow. Her dress: none. Her breasts, firm but hardly overregulated, jutted forth to present areolas the size of campaign lapel buttons. I told her I found her blatant emotional appeal enticing. Well, she said, it's only a week until the election.

Walking home along the waterfront we witnessed a shootout between supporters of Bozo and supporters of the incumbent, armed with rapid-fire urban assault rifles of the variety that her candidate would ban and mine would restrict. The gunners hid behind steel-reinforced campaign signs staked into the small patches of dirt where trees refused to grow. Vote Trust. Vote Change. Yes On Measure No. No On Measure Yes. If You Love Children, Vote For Guns. We dove through the crossfire and ducked down a side alley, where we each made fumbling attempts to shield the other's body with our own. Everything was going well until she told me to get on my knees and beg.

"Beg for what exactly?" I asked, because I try always to keep abreast of the issues.

"Beg for the following: entitlement programs, educational excellence, freedom of speech, freedom of choice, freedom of religion, honesty in government, absolution from sin, a chicken in every pot, and an end to global warming."

"You sadist!" I cried. She left in tears, and I walked home alone, feeling dirty, feeling used. And yet ... somehow, secretly thrilled.

◉   ◉   ◉

I arrived home to find a steaming, smelly pile of campaign literature puddled in the front hall. Vandals had stuffed it through my mail slot. I fetched a sponge and some ammonia from the kitchen, but when I bent to sop up the mess, I caught a whiff of her perfume, the aroma of her campaign. Eau de Franco, a distinctive blend of patchouli and snake oil. My mother wore it when I was in high school. The nose, they say, is the quickest path to a man's vote.

I carefully scooped up a slate card and sniffed the pungent aroma. I had forgotten the smell of ink that wasn't soy-based. I picked up another flier, lifted my shirt and rubbed the warm, slimy propaganda across my nipples. The mild sting was titillating. My mind seethed with images of an all-nude hot-pork-wrestling match between the left and right wings of the Supreme Court. I saw Rheinquist, his tight red face and tortured lips quivering with each slap of a marinated ham hock on the prostrate, wrinkled buttocks of Clarence Thomas. As I slid my fingers past my belt I imagined that down the street a busload of children from a poor congressional district was driving past the shiny new astrodome, when out from the revolving toll gates poured a thousand American Gladiators, steroids dripping from their freshly shaven glistening backs. I saw them lay siege to the bus with enormous Q-Tips and tennis ball cannons. One by one the windows exploded inwards, the children were pulled out and passed, arm over arm, to the stainless steel feeder bin of the giant threshing device, stenciled "VOTE HERE". America needs these children's testosterone. America needs their skin. American needs their votes. American needs ...

I ejaculated across a family photo of the incumbent, his family arms around his smiling wife Barbara and

18

daughter Nancy. A thin string of semen separated his son Bobby, a young man my age who stood more off to the left. The layout artist had cropped the son's shoulder. His expression seemed to say: please get this over with.

◉   ◉   ◉

During the final week of the campaign, all citizens were advised to remain in their sealed rooms, and to keep their nerve gas antidote kits constantly beside them, and to watch always their TVs. But on voting night I ventured out with a small group of Bozo supporters from my block who were keen to assess the situation. There was me, Jerry from party headquarters, Sam and Mitch, a little shrimpy guy named Louis, two older women named Donna and Christie, another guy from the party named Anguello, who brought his three year old daughter Sue, a teenage hippie girl also named Sue, her boyfriend from El Salvador who's name I forgot, my next-door neighbor Clay, and his boy scout troop. We met at my apartment, put on our noses and our floppy shoes, and piled into the Honda. Nobody spoke much, we were all too worried. The polls had Doubt at 37%, Hope at 36.5%, with the third-party feeling of Uncertainty trailing at 20%, and with 6.5% of voters undecided. Pundits predicted that for our side to turn things around we would need campaign donations to buy 720,000 more votes, or else the incumbent would have to throw up on another world leader. There was also a disturbing rumor in circulation that Bozo didn't really like children. None of us knew what to think or what to expect.

The streets in our neighborhood were deserted. Every house was slathered with signs. Some people's front lawns had been badly tilled in scenarios where lawn sign commandos from the warring parties had tried to crowd each others' signs out of view. At the intersection of Placid and Liberty we saw a charred and bombed-out loudspeaker car, stalled and dead but still hissing static, a victim of sniper fire. It was so badly disfigured we couldn't tell if it was one of ours or one of theirs. We left a rubber nose on the hood ornament and got away from there.

We decided we weren't drunk enough, so we stopped by a bar that was known to be partisan, the Leaning Booth. The others crowded around the television, waiting for news from the front. The pope has endorsed the incumbent, it said, and Madonna has endorsed Bozo. I had a martini. I had another martini. I had a third martini. I thought about Trust, Character, Change. I didn't like any of them. I had a fourth martini. Each martini olive had two spears — one sword and one American flag. I had a fourth martini, again. I now had five swords and five flags. Once upon a time we fought a war for freedom. When was that? Where was I? I had another flag. Six Flags. The incumbent campaigned there just last week. It was on the TV, he addressed the paying audience and the elves. Talking about Freedom, Trust, Character, Safety. Bozo was to speak at Disneyland later that day about Happy, Friendly, Children, Wonderful. Mickey Mouse, employed by loyalists but sympathetic to the cause, was not allowed by his superiors to speak at the event, and had to introduce Bozo through mime. He had his little gloves on, he had another martini and he mimed a scene in the voting booth, where the lever was too high up and he had to climb on the shoulders of children. Mickey Mouse climbed on the shoulders of children. The children were not smiling. The children were forced into the scenario by their forefathers. What were they thinking? Did they understand why this is all necessary? When the bomb went off under the podium, did they hear the noise? Did they feel the impact? Did Mickey? Or did it all just wash over them like a bad but overpowering idea, like a loud commercial on a big TV. They didn't ask for it. Who asked for it? Why can't we get what we want?

I don't remember where I voted that night, or who I voted for. I only remember the lever going down, the sound of the latch and my legs falling out from under me. 👁

ADVERTISEMENT

MSL is now selling by mail LARGE MONITOR
LIZARDS. These lizards are very large and sprightly
when shipped. Your PUNK FRIENDS may want to
buy one for their bathroom. We also offer LOUD
SCREECHING MUSIC. Your PUNK FRIENDS will
be impressed when you play it for them and it is totally
UNLISTENABLE. They will think you have rarefied
tastes. You are authorized to duplicate these LOUD
SCREECHING sounds for your punk friends, so that
they may sophisticate themselves at your expense.
MSL also sells T-SHIRTS advertising the fact that you
are one of the suckers who has fallen into our trap. It
is certain that when enough people wear MSL
T-SHIRTS, they will be considered FASHIONABLE,
and those people who wore them first will impress
their PUNK FRIENDS with their advanced sense of
fashionability. MSL also sells ZINES written by people
who need spare money for T-SHIRTS, LOUD
SCREECHING MUSIC and MONITOR LIZARDS.
MSL ZINES are guaranteed against MUTILATION.
If you receive a ZINE from MSL that is
MUTILATED, other than during shipping and/or by
MONITOR LIZARDS, MSL guarantees that we will
do something about it and it will all be OKAY. MSL
sells all of the above merchandise at BULK
DISCOUNT to stores that share the MSL philosophy
of "selling our merchandise, in exchange for money, to
people who seem to want to buy it for some reason."
This way you can make money off your friends, like we
do. MSL produces the MSL CATALOG, which lists
all of these OFFERINGS and also contains insightful
and/or humorous ZINE-LIKE CONTENT, which is

how we get away with charging you a DOLLAR and a stamp and an envelope. Send self-addressed stamped envelope plus a DOLLAR to:

SPECIAL RIPPING-YOU-OFF OFFER
MYKLE SYSTEMS LABS
5536 NE 27TH AVE
PORTLAND OREGON 97211-6230

UHF

I went over to Mark's place to watch The Simpsons but we couldn't really pick up Fox properly on his TV because: apparently there's some new cellular phone antenna that they just put up on the roof of the church two blocks away, the First Chinese Mennonite, and it's not supposed to do this but it ruins all reception of the UHF channels between about 14 and about 35, including of course TV20 which is where we get Fox. The neighbors have all been talking to each other about it, and to the cellular company, and I guess there's supposed to be this technical grievance process that they have to go through before they can get it fixed They'd probably all be raising more of a shitstorm about it if it wasn't for this sort of delicate side issue, specifically the Chinese Mennonites sort of feel like the whole neighborhood is against them ever since this really awful cross-burning episode which happened well over a year ago, and which everybody in town absolutely condemned, and which was traced not even to the local Klan (we do have one) but to a couple of junkie high school kids who had some incomprehensible personal beef to unfurl on the lawn of the First Chinese Mennonite. So now people are going over and talking to the old reverend guy who's in charge of the place and who doesn't speak English but communicates through his son, and they're very nicely and politely explaining to him this issue with their TV reception versus the antenna, which the reverend kind of pretends to understand, he smiles, but he doesn't even own a TV and probably has not ever even been exposed to that kind of audiovisual worldly temptation in the orphanage to monastery to ecumenical college in

24

Bavaria someplace to boatload of Chinese Mennonites coming up the Willamette river like fifty years ago to buy some land and spread the word story of his life. At any rate TV is not a big part of this guy's world, although he does seem to enjoy this new ultra-slim StarTac cellular phone that he likes to talk to people on, I don't know who he talks to, maybe God. It seems that while he doesn't automatically have the legal right to ruin local UHF reception from the steeple of his little white church there — said steeple now decorated with three white bulbous things with sloppy red Mennonite crosses painted on them but with the Motorola logo also still visible, and one blinking spire that goes up like 30 feet beyond the existing spire and certainly does appear to lend the building that extra little pinch of spiritual receiving power — but neither does anybody in the area have any right to do anything about it, and it's seeming more and more unlikely that this issue will be resolved in our lifetime, but:

Mark said "Come over anyway" because what they now receive on the UHF channel is kind of weirdly interesting as well, plus we can always sit around and hit the bong and play guitar and generally hang out even if The Simpsons don't show up. The weirdly interesting thing is you can hear the dialogue of The Simpsons pretty well most of the time, but on the screen — which is just has this little 13" portable job from the early 80's, with fake-metal anodized case and huge rabbit ears and a huge UHF coil, such that it actually gets better reception than most modern TVs, says Mark, though he also can't afford to buy most modern TVs due to a familiar wife kid car mortgage situation, but anyway — on the screen there seems to be, as far as we can make out, some sort of satellite pay-porno channel leaking over. It's very faint and staticky. But occasionally, like if someone in another room holds a metal spatula in midair, cheesy music and loud moaning come blaring across, and it's either bad synthesizer wallpaper music or else sad jazz fusion music, plus either sex swearing stuff or else just panting and wet slapping noises ... but Mark was quick to point out to me that there's more than just this whacked superimposition of cartoons and porno that was fast making this his favorite channel (I was actually sort of wondering whether he was getting into the kinky aspect of this strange dialogue: Homer says some dumb Homer thing and then Marge says "well Homey, you could always just FUCK ME IN THE ASS IN THE ASS LIKE A MAN WITH YOUR FAT friends back at the plant who HEY BARB, THIS IS JOE AGAIN —"

To explain: besides the fuzzy pay-porno and besides the Simpsons, there's also local cellular phone traffic bleeding in to this same channel, channel 20. And it seems for some reason that it's always either voices in Chinese and with a lot of laughing, or else it's this one particular guy. And Mark said that he sometimes leaves the TV on tuned to 20 just to wait for this one particular guy's conversation, whose name is Joe and he must live around here, he makes six or seven calls every evening around the same time, and they're to various different people but mostly to either this woman named Barb, who it's pretty clear he's somewhere in the divorce process with, or else to his lawyer, named Mel, who's also involved in that process and with whom Joe's (apparently) conspiring to get a really big, one-sided and unfair divorce settlement out of said Barb. While we listened to this three-way audio confusion field together, and these details of someone else's divorce, and cartoons, and sex, I asked Mark if, like hypothetically, he thinks that it's okay for a given person to be listening in on the private phone conversations of some other given hypothetical person, ethically speaking, but Mark did point out that a) these high-power waves of electromagnetic information were currently travelling through him, myself, his daughter Emma, and his wife when she's home, actually penetrating all of our bodies, and nobody asked any of us if this was okay, and that asking us to, in effect, ignore these waves inside our own selves and not look at them out of respect for the privacy of unknown wave-generating individuals was perhaps unreasonable or unfair or un-something-else, and anyway the point is 2) they took away our fucking Simpsons.

And to make things even more entertaining, Joe has a speech impediment, a sort of a sloppy S noise that perhaps isn't so pronounced in person but after he speaks into his (presumably) cellular phone and that gets amplified and transmitted and (presumably) re-amplified by the bulbous antenna nodules on the First Chinese Mennonite church which is only four houses down from Mark's, and retransmitted, and then that signal invades the circuitry of this early-80s TV set that is designed to receive something completely else, and then gets re-re-amplified and run through the tiny TV speaker, by that time it sounds like a huge burst of square-wave noise every time he says the letter S, which he comically says pretty often. Some people who lisp avoid using the words that they can't say but this guy Joe seems to overcompensate, for instance his pet names for his ex-wife-to-be Barb include: Sweetie, Sugar, babycakeS, SunShine, and (a favorite for some reason) SweetcheekS. Mark & I can't imagine what it must have been like for that poor woman to be married to this guy and having him spitting all over her all the time ... he also has a bunch of irritating phrases that he likes to use, most of which have strong S sounds all through them, like "So what you're Sayin' iS" and "So here'S how I See it" and "So-So" and "I See, I See."

After a couple of bonghits each you can imagine how funny this might get, even compared to the Simpsons. But last night it got sort of out of control, when we were picking up this conversation between Joe and Mel, the lawyer, and we heard the two of them sort of joking about how they were going to leave Barb penniless, with nothing, and never let her see her kid again and so on, and then kind of in passing they were talking about how happier everybody (but she) would be if something would go wrong with the brakes in her car. (Which is a Jaguar apparently — another clue indicating that Joe and/or Barb have a lot of money. Yet another such clue is that Joe for some reason prefers to use his cell phone even though he's apparently calling from his house where he could use the normal phone and save a bundle.) Mark, upon hearing of this planned duplicity, got suddenly very pissed off and intense. Like night and day it was, one moment we were just laughing about it all and the next he was really wanting to find this guy Joe and ... yell at him or something. Me personally, I figured it would be a better idea to just tape-record some of these conversations and send them somehow to Barb, if we could figure out where she lived. But the thing is, all of these conversations were interspersed with dirty sex talk (mostly from these women who push 900 sex numbers in the commercial breaks and the one phrase that they seem to say over and over is STICK YOUR PHONE IN MY CUNT!) and also bits of The Simpsons (I think the plot was something about Mr. Burns regressing to a past life, while Homer gets involved in a men's drumming group or therapy or something, but at this point I sort of lost track) and I don't know if the point would come across clearly on tape. But anyway like I said we were pretty stoned ... and I forget who came up with the idea but before too long we had collected together all of the extension cords in the house and hauled the TV set out on to the porch.

Emma, Mark's kid, was kind of pissed off because we had to steal the extension cord that runs from the garage out into the back yard and up into the tree where she has her totally killer tree house (which Mark and I built), and up there she has an old TV of her own (which Mark and I almost killed ourselves hauling

up there) that she had been watching some bullshit
program about horses on, but once she saw that we
were out on an expedition she wanted to come along,
even though it was getting late. But it seemed like a
good idea to me because God knows it's hard getting
kids interested in anything adults like to do. And also
I figured that if Mark had any unstable or (ick) violent
plans in mind — which I doubt because he's usually a
sweetheart — that he wouldn't try any of it in front of
his 8-year-old daughter who he's normally kind of
self-conscious around. And I wasn't sure if we would
be able to use the volume of the signal received to
triangulate the source like we planned, because TVs
have auto-gain-controls in them, and even if it did
work I figured it would just lead us towards the First
Chinese Mennonite and what would that tell us? But
you know, when you're stoned you do dumb things.
So we hooked everything up, and wound the extension
cords around and around Emma and showed her how
to twirl around clockwise to take the line in and
counterclockwise to let it out. Then we powered up
the set, and it was a bit awkward because it seemed,
from that position and collection of hard-to-isolate
reception variables, the porno channel came through
louder and clearer than ever, while The Simpsons were
plowed under the snow, and Joe wasn't on the phone at
that moment.

It was sort of a sketchy situation at that point. We're
all sitting on the front porch, and we're watching these
two women on the TV sort of taking each other's
clothes off, the volume is turned up, little Lisa Simpson

is unwittingly entangled in an adult consensual lesbian sex event, and there's Mark's daughter standing next to us by the TV, tied up in orange and yellow extension cords. I mean people don't really bug or interlope upon their neighbors much in the neighborhood where we live, we all respect each other's privacy most of the time, but Mark & I became kind of intensely paranoid that someone might see us on the porch and get a wrong idea. Emma, for her part, appeared to find the porno kind of boring, and I gather from what Mark tells me that she knows all about sex already and thinks it's incredibly, incredibly gross. But still ... we were about to chicken out and move everything back inside when suddenly we heard the string of little beeps that meant that Joe was placing a call.

So we were off. Joe began talking now to Barb, and he was really laying on the sugar, perhaps because in our last episode we learned that Barb's lawyer (Laura) had sent some communique to Joe's lawyer (Mel) that had him and Joe a little bit concerned, and I guess Joe was supposed to sweet-talk her into just not doing anything, in a legal sort of way, while the two of them (Joe and Mel) got some sort of litigation ready that was supposed to, in Joe's terms, "Staple her to the Seeling," financially speaking. So there was Joe, showing his vulnerable side on the phone with Barb ... meanwhile there were Mark & I, standing out in the middle of the cul-de-sac with Emma giggling and spinning around in circles on the porch, letting out more of this long ratty string of tied-together extension cords. We walked twenty paces in the direction of the church, and the signal started to break up more. "Colder," Mark said, which surprised me and contradicted my original theory about where the signal was originating from. And we walked twenty paces in another direction, off 90 degrees from our first path, Mark holding the TV against his chest with both hands ("portable" TVs from that era weigh about 40 pounds) and me watching it, walking backwards facing him, outside in the dark, with the volume turned all the way up and these occasional moans and swells of porn-soundtrack interspersed with Joe, The Simpsons, and blurry fuzz. Colder. We moved out into the intersection, Emma still twirling around, and Mark says "Shit! Colder!" Then we head back towards the house in frustration, but then the signal gets warmer, definitely. Joe meanwhile is doing a real number on Barb, I can't believe she's falling for this but I guess she went as far as to marry the guy at some point so she must be a sucker. His big soliloquy goes "SweetcheekS, all I'm Saying iS we Shouldn't Say no, never, nothing. We Should Say, you know ... Something! Someday, poSSibly ... I miSS you Sugar ..." et cetera.

We strung all of the wire back through the living room, through the kitchen, and out the back patio into Mark's yard, which is pretty large and which isn't separated from the other yards by fences, yet, although there is one guy down the block who's installing fence posts and the whole neighborhood is up in arms about it because: this guy is some rich yuppie who bought the house a year ago and still never talks to his neighbors except to ask tactless questions about their property and their equity in it, like he's waiting for all of the rest of us to move away so he can own the whole block, and apparently also he doesn't recycle. But anyway, we start walking out across the lawn and the signal is getting warmer, warmer still. Emma at this point has given up trying to keep the cord wound and is just playing with it, whipping it up and down, sending waves along its length. Mark follows the signal across his yard, across his next-door neighbor's yard, and runs out of extension cord halfway through the yard after that, which is the yard of the Bad Taste People who have covered their back yard with tiny ugly green concrete frogs from Fred Meyer, and flimsy plastic-resin injection molded lawn furniture, also from Fred Meyer, which is all fallen over because it won't stand up on anything but concrete, and which is laced with glistening slug trails. Also they have a dwarf picnic bench, also pre-fab also from Fred Meyer, and also they have a 50-foot extension cord hanging on a little hanger under their back porch next to their lawn mower, which cord Mark immediately grabs and splices into the power line. He doesn't even stop to consider not doing it or asking first. When he gets done and turns the TV back on, the signal is so hot that every sibilant S is like pressurized air escaping from a car lift, and Mark at this point is laughing and shouting "We're reading you Joe! We're picking you up loud and clear!" The extra extension cord takes us out of the Bad Taste Zone and across another yard and into the yard where the aforementioned fence is being dug. There's lots of other high-end landscaping stuff beginning to happen there. Bags of high-grade horseshit are stacked in a pile along with sacks of cedar chips, there's a couple cords of cedar deck lumber fresh from the mill, and behind it all there's a pit dug where I guess they're going to put in a hot-tub or a pond or something. So we're standing there, we've run our of extension cord, Mark is peering around in the dark, pointing the blue-blinky TV light around and looking for the free extension cord that he's expecting to find in every neighbor's yard apparently. Emma is just looking up at the house. I follow her gaze to see that there's one light on in an upstairs window and one silhouette is talking on the phone, and it penetrates my stoned brain that yeah, this is probably Joe's yard, that's probably Joe up there talking! This looks like his kind of yard. Mark's obviously had the same thought, because he's looking up there too, and now he's silent, and we're all standing in the yard, looking up at the window, listening to Barb's voice as she's sort of letting her emotional guard down and confessing embarrassing things, it's become black outside, the snow from the TV is casting this light that's now blue, now pink, and then I hear this weird sound, a buzzing, clicking sound, and I smell sparks .. and I look at Mark and see that he's sort of shaking ... he's being electrocuted! I grab a sack of cedar chips ... he's standing in the mud and he's got no shoes on ... I swing the plastic sack of cedar chips at the TV he's holding, to knock it out of his arms, and the sack breaks open when it hits and the chips fly all over him, he topples backwards slowly like a bookshelf, still clutching the TV, but when he hits the ground the TV falls out of his grasp and into the pit. Mark is lying on the ground, panting, he's saying "aaaaaaaaa" but he's also kind of laughing ... Emma doesn't seem to understand what's just happened ... but you can't hear anything very well because the TV is still on in the bottom of the pit, and somehow either because reception is better down there or because the volume knob got bumped or because of the acoustics of the hole itself, the volume is really immensely loud, public-address level it seems, it echoes, and apparently while all this drama was happening, Joe said something wrong and Barb is now calling him on his bullshit, and now they're having a full-fledged vicious argument, and Joe is calling Barb a Sneak and a Slut and a Sybil and saying he's going to cruSh her aSS into the Sidewalk! And a floodlight goes on over the back yard of the Bad Taste people two doors down.

Mark gets up onto his knees, he's panting and feeling himself all over but, amazingly, he seems to be conscious and perhaps not badly hurt, but his mood has totally changed. "Definitely time to bail," he says, and just then we see Joe's silhouette slide open the upstairs window and peer out at us, and we just start hauling ass as fast as we can, Mark grabbing Emma's arm and half-lifting her off the ground. Halfway back to the house Mark stops to try and undo the last link of the extension cord, and it takes him a little while because he also knotted it, and only then I notice: at the Bad Taste House some figure is standing on the back porch, holding I think a bottle of something in one hand, just quietly watching and listening.
We can all hear Joe hanging up on Barb, dialing 911 and talking to some operator there. All he can say is

"There'S treSpaSSerS on my premiSeS!" and she keeps asking him if he needs an ambulance, or is there a crime in progress, or is his life in danger, and he says "EaveSdropperS in my yard! They're liStening on my Sellphone!" and she's asking him over and over, Are you injured? Have you been shot? I swear I can hear whoever it is up on the Bad Taste Porch laughing. Then it goes instantly dark and quiet, and Mark grabs the free end of the cord and we all make a quick fucking getaway. 👁

What Jack Was Like:

Some people are like cliffs that you can jump off of
and fall to your death on the dry jagged rocks below.
Some people are like long hallways you can shout
down and hear the distant echo of your own voice
coming back at you, but no other signs of life. Some
people are like albino ferrets that hop up and down
when they're excited and that are cute but kind of
bad-smelling. Some people are like dwarves, in fact
they actually are dwarves. Some people are unable to
cope in normal society and yet rise to the occasion in
conditions of pure survival. Some people have extra
nipples. Some people owe me money. Jack was all of
these things, and more.

He lived in a hole in a shoe in a forest in a can, in
France, in the summer, in June in debt in a constant
state of doubt, on some land near a continent with
oceans next to it somewhere north of Antarctica. He
had a certain indescribable something. He kept it on a
string looped around his waist. He liked cats, falafel,
long walks on the beach, honesty, Grand Marinier, his
mom, films, breathing, himself, food that didn't have
giant quivering gobs of pus and fungus with tiny
eyeballs and tentacles and raspy teeth crawling all over
it, large unexpected government benefit checks, cheese,
and people with names beginning with vowels. His
turn-offs included: nuclear winter, human feces, being
beaten about the face and neck with the barrel of a
large automatic pistol, rape, chewing on tin foil, food
that did have giant quivering gobs of pus and fungus
with tiny eyeballs and tentacles and raspy teeth
crawling all over it, court appearances, drowning,

38

cancer, canned vegetables, snowboarding, moments of
sudden, unshakable and complete comprehension of
one's own mortality, artificial breasts, lard in Mexican
cooking, man's inhumanity to man and beets. He had
at various times in his life been a lifeguard, a mailman,
a boxer, a telephone sanitizer, a build-maintenance
engineer, a dental hygienist, a sucker, a straight-man, a
second-story man, a minor functionary, a middle
manager, a bum, a dwarf, a dwarf-bum, a dental-
dwarf-hygienist-middle-bum-manager-engineer, a
contractor, a consultant, an activist, an anarchist, an
anaesthesiologist, a picador, a conquistador, a barrista,
an underclass, a phalanx, a junta, a soccer team, the
upper twenty floors of both towers of the World Trade
Center in New York, an ant, a microbe, a giant
quivering gob of pus and fungus with tiny eyeballs and
tentacles and raspy teeth that crawled along the ocean
floor in search of food, or companionship, or
stimulating entertainment, or heroism, or just to end it
all and see what happens next, and he had also been
the driver of a school bus full of blind orphan
quadriplegics on the way to a lacrosse match against a
school of deaf test-tube amnesiacs, as part of an
intramural handicapped lacrosse program funded in
part by the President's Council on Physical Fitness,
when a sudden mechanical failure in the transaxle
caused everybody's heads to detach from their necks
and fall off onto the floor and roll up and down the
center aisle bumping against one another like bowling
balls do in the bowling ball return mechanism exit
chute storage groove thing that they have at bowling
alleys, and understandably he had been scarred by this

experience so he didn't do that any more. When I met him, he was dead. I haven't seen him recently. I often wonder where he is, what's he's doing, whether he's finally gotten over the trauma of that horrible day, or that other trauma of that other horrible day when he woke up on the ocean floor to find giant quivering gobs of pus and fungus with tiny eyeballs and tentacles and raspy teeth chewing on him, and he said: "Hey, stop that, cut that out!" and they looked at him with their tiny eyeballs assuming an expression that said: like, who's this guy? Like as if *he* was the one who was interloping and being rude, and presumptuous, and not these horrible unreal parasitic pus-fungus creatures that were touching him with their hideous clammy tentacles and digesting his flesh, and it was all very awkward. I wonder if he ever found love. I wonder if he's still a dwarf. Maybe someday he'll call me. 👁

My Armenia

I often find myself at parties, drunk and cornered, or
else simply cornered, by someone who wants to ask me
getting-to-know-you type questions. Where am I
from? Where did I go to school? What do I do for a
living? Oh, really? Maybe they find me attractive,
maybe they feel some social obligation to be chatty.
Either way I find these questions tedious, and the
answers more so. It's fortunate for these inquisitive
party types that I am a professional liar, er, I mean,
author of fiction.

"Where are you from?" is a popular question, and I
have been asked this one many times. Where I'm from
is a long story that's not particularly easy to tell or
interesting to hear. Some time ago, I began lying
about this, just to get things going. "Armenia," I say.
"My parents moved to the U.S. shortly after I was
born."

"Armenia? Really? I've never been there!" Their eyes
light up. People want to hear all about it. "What part
of Armenia are you from?" As if they've heard of the
different parts of Armenia. "Do you speak Armenian
fluently?" "No," I answer, "Armenians generally speak
French and Uzbek. But I speak only Uzbek."

What do you eat in Armenia? Camels, mostly. Oh,
are there many deserts there? No, they aren't desert
camels, they are plains camels. And how are the camels
prepared? They are prepared with many native spices,
including saffron, tunic, and monticello.

How fascinating! Tell us more! And so I have bamboozled many strangers with stories about my non-homeland. Occasionally someone who has heard something about Armenia will interject a morsel of relevant trivia. In these cases, I usually explain that my people are Southern Armenians, who have a very different culture from the Northern Armenian culture that is so frequently portrayed in your Hollywood movies.

Armenia is the answer to all irritating questions. For instance: I am in the habit of wandering aimlessly around antiquarian bookstores, because I like old spines. I never ever buy anything. I really don't think this is such a crime, but book-thropes who hope to subtly unwelcome me from their shops usually begin their efforts with some sort of inquiry along the lines of first "Ehem," then "is there something in particular that you're looking for?" When dealing with these unpleasant people I usually do my best to send them on some sort of hunt:

"Yes, in fact, do you have any Armenian poetry?"

Usually the proprietor is very certain that they don't have any such stuff. But you know, booksellers really can't keep that good a track of their stock. Say: "A friend of mine told me that he saw a very nice collection of Armenian poetry here just one month ago," and then they will get all tizzified looking for it. Insist that they search thoroughly. I used to think there was actually no such thing as Armenian poetry, but once I got a call from some antiquarian bookman who had noted my interests and made me write my number down. Months later he left an excited message on my machine pertaining to a collection he had located quite by accident, known to be available for sale, of Armenian love poems in translation. I called back to ask him whether the poems were in sonnet form. They were not. Now I ask for Armenian sonnets specifically.

One fine cocktail I found myself surrounded by a trio of young, attractive female college students — my favorite kinds of people, really — and was asked about my background. Upon my reply, I was informed that they were all Armenian too. The three of them were the first Armenians I ever met, and in my haste to impress them and create a bond, I unfortunately forgot that all my Armenian knowledge was drunken fabrication. I stumbled through an interrogation. What city in Armenia? Ludou. Where is that? In the south. Do you play Kratsky Tolny? I love to when the weather is fair. Do you know where a good dolma can be had? No, I have never had a dolma like my dear dead grandmother's. (Much commiseration here.) So, are you spatni or strashny?

Eh?

You know, are you red or blue? It's okay, they said. We aren't political. Just curious.

I launched into an oration concerning the international brotherhood of humankind and the need to erase borders and heal broken scars. They applauded my sentiments, and then asked again, this time most intently: Spatni or Strashny?

I said I was half-and-half. My mother was spatni, my father strashny. They paled. One of them turned and stormed away. Another one said, "I'm sorry, I didn't know. I don't mean to embarrass you." But after that they looked at me like I was a troll, and the conversation returned to safe topics, and then petered out completely. 👁

Metrophobia

Everybody knows you can't just go out walking around.
There's places in Northeast where they'll just come
running out of their houses with guns, looking for
meat. Anyway, there's a huge speed trap out that way
— the cops there are real rednecks. Downtown you
have to watch out for feral cats. There's packs of them,
some have rabies. Don't — DO NOT — flash your
headlights at someone who hasn't turned them on! I
read on the Internet that there's a new gang thing —
the city is full of gangs and drugs, especially in the
Northeast — where they drive around with the
headlights off & carjack the first car that flashes at
them. Carjackings are up this year ... but God knows
it's not safe to just walk around. I just hope we can
keep all that stuff out of this neighborhood. Yesterday
a big Oldsmobile parked right in front of my neighbor
Mabel's house — they didn't look like anybody she'd
know — I just didn't know what to do! I was about to
call 911, but then I remembered that I had heard the
police will only answer one 911 call per telephone per
month, because the crime problem is so dramatic, and
I thought "What if they go away when the police
arrive, but then come back afterwards? And what if
the police want to come in, and they decide I look
suspicious, and they search my apartment and find my
stash? Or they just decide to plant something on me?"
So I went down to the basement with the mobile
phone — I hoped to God they didn't have a one of
those scanners! — and I listened, and I waited. The
phone has emergency buttons programmed on it, red
buttons, so I can dial 911 with only one press instead
of three, or else I can call Animal Control, Poison

Control or my sister in Medford, instantly. I was
down there for a couple of hours, just listening for
trouble and watching all of the horrible little bugs we
have down there. Honestly — little silverfish, spiders,
they get in through the cracks. I never imagined there
were so many. I finally got down on hands & knees
with a brick and started crushing them, one after the
other, until I was pretty sure I got them all.

When I went back upstairs the Oldsmobile had snuck
away. But then I noticed there was some sort of flyer
stuck through the mail slot, and then I remembered:
they haven't caught the Unabomber yet, have they? 👁

Letter to the Manufacturers of
Alley Katz Katz Food

Dear sirs: I would like to thank and congratulate you on the quality of your cat repellent, Alley Katz Katz Food, which I've been using for the last few months to keep these meowing pests out of my home. Never have I seen animals so transfixed, held firmly at bay by an invisible feline wall of distaste. I am writing also to inquire whether you market a slug and snail food, preferably in the same cheese and liver flavor that you claim Katz Krave, or else in a configuration that might analogously nauseate slithering pests. (I imagine you employ experts in this area.) (Lettuce and salt peanuts, perhaps?)

Finally, I would also inquire whether you could recommend a company that manufactures edible food for cats, in case I suffer a change of heart.

Yrs, E. Tarantula, fellow cat hater.

◉   ◉   ◉

Sirs: in inconspicuous lettering on the back of my box of Alley Katz Katz Food, you warn that a temporary period of appetite loss is normal when attempting to feed your products to Katz. How long does this period last, in the normal case? I opened a bag of your Liver 'N Onion flavored product two weeks ago, and have been unable to stomach either of these foods in their unprocessed form ever since. My cats, meanwhile, have begun to eat their own litter and beg from passing children. Also: you warn that if this condition persists for over a month, some other cause (malnutrition?) may be suspected and a veterinarian ought to be consulted. Call me premature: I have spoken with my regular vet, Frida, who has suggested that I investigate the meat over meat by-products ratio of your Katz Food. Apparently when this ratio approaches zero, so does one's cat.

Please advise, E. Tarantula, vegetarian adept

◉　　◉　　◉

Sirs: a spot of confusion surrounding your product, to wit: on the front of your package you picture, seated on an ersatz fence, a furry creature of feline build, healthy in appearance and cat-like in all outward aspects, but apparently able to metabolize Alley Katz Katz Food for nutritional value. I suspect the confusion here is that this creature is a "Katz," perhaps some bizarre Australian offshoot from the evolutionary tree of the common housecat, with entirely foreign dietary needs, and what I suspected as mere post-literacy on the part of your writing staff was actually a subtle but important distinction overlooked by the stock clerks at my local market. I should be relieved to know if this is true, and out of curiosity and ignorance, what other toxins is this creature able to absorb, and could one cohabit with humans? I've considered procuring a goat to clear out the blown waste that collects in my yard. Perhaps a Katz would be less obtrusive, and also able to dispose of this mistakenly purchased bag of Alley Katz Katz Food (tofu double liver flavor), which my garbagemen refuse to collect for fear of being fined.

Inquisitively yours, E. Tarantula.

◉ ◉ ◉

Dear Alley Katz Katz Food Kreators: Your Krispy
Kroutons of Krunchy Katzfood Kause my Katz to
Kough up Krust! Klearly I am Koncerned! If you
Kontinue to Klaim that Katz, or any Kreatures, Krave
this Krud you Kall Katfood, you risk being Kalled in
by the Kops and the ASPKA on Kharges of Kruelty!

no Kidding! E.T.

◉ ◉ ◉

Dear Sirs: ever since I tried to feed your food to my cat
Splotch, she has denied me affection, companionship,
and even the smallest of courtesies. Normally carefree
and energetic, she now paces absently from room to
room, or merely gazes out the window, her eyes
betraying not the slightest awareness of her
surroundings. Sometimes in the night she cries out in
long, baleful meows as if recoiling from a memory too
terrible for her little kitty brain to encompass.
For how many weeks is this behavior considered
normal? 👁

I Saw This Movie

I saw this movie where the plot was: everything catches on fire and starts to explode. Then it continues to explode, in a series of increasingly huge explosions, until eventually mountains are exploding, and then the earth explodes and then the sun explodes. It had George Clooney and Gwyneth Paltrow in it. I hear they're already working on a sequel. Speaking of sequels, there's this one I saw the trailer for called Twisterconda, where this gigantic computer-generated anaconda starts threatening the inhabitants of this 20-story condominium out on the prairie in North Dakota, and then this gigantic computer-generated twister tornado comes speeding towards the same building, and then the twister and the anaconda sort of duke it out in a big final fight scene. It's got Leonardo DiCaprio and Pierce Brosnan and Gwyneth Paltrow, it ought to be pretty good. I also saw a trailer for this movie called The Odd Couple, and I guess it's based on some old TV show where there's this space station orbiting the earth that gets infiltrated by hideous space-anacondas and these two guys who live in the space station have to save the earth, and there's a hull breach, and some laser gunfights, and also I guess there's this subplot that they really hate each other. It's got George Clooney and Bruce Willis in it, and one of the space anacondas is played by Gwyneth Paltrow. I'm looking forward to that one. I also read in Entertainment Preview that there's some movie coming up that's got Bruce Willis, Gwyneth Paltrow, Willie Smith, Tommy Lee Jones, Sissy Spacek, Jack Nicholson and Cher in it. That ought to be pretty good. It's about some disease that makes people bleed out of their anuses and die really disgustingly. I think it's called Fasciitis: Final Conflict but I'm not sure how that's pronounced, "fasciitis." And there's this Arnold Schwartzenegger movie I heard is almost done, where Arnold Schwartzenegger plays the President of the United States, and these alien monsters who disguise themselves as Arabs sneak into the White House and take everybody hostage, and start running the country, and I guess they do a bad job or something because then the President, who's trapped in the Oval Office, has to escape and sneak around in all the secret passageways that only the President knows about, and kill all of the Arab space aliens, only they attach this deadly energy bomb to the United States Constitution, and the President has to disarm the bomb before it blows up the Constitution and the whole country reverts to a loose affiliation of nation-states, and then gets annexed by this other planet of the Arab space aliens who are apparently all Communists. It seems kind of stupid but I'll probably go see it. 👁

Two Eggs

I would like two eggs. I wold like the eggs to be identical in every way, genetically that is, I mean to say that I would like two eggs laid by the same hen, simultaneously if that is possible or else one right after the other. They ought also to be weighed and measured for any deformity, and a suitable stress-test should be devised in order to screen out weakness that might later affect the meal. Several two-egg candidate pairs should be assembled just in case something bad happens.

I would like the first egg scrambled, via ultrasound if possible. If there is no suitable ultrasonic egg scrambling apparatus, you may use twelve turns with a sterilized wooden spoon, heating the egg over a PH-neutral panlike cooking surface that is perfectly flat. Please take care to avoid excessive lumps.

The second of my eggs should be buried in a pot of earth, PH-neutral earth, for a period of three days and three nights, the third of those nights coinciding with the full moon. Then, at midnight on the third night, I would like you to stand nude in a cemetery with tar smeared across your bare torso, holding the potted egg aloft, and I would like you to chant "Imalla Assaka Loba Doba Egg Foontella!" and then unearth the egg and prepare it in the usual fashion, as outlined above.

Of course I would like sausages with my eggs. The Aeronautical Meat Sciences Board publishes a set of detailed specifications of various sizes and textures of sausage. The sausage I am hoping for is described in

AMSB Document 01-3382-Sausage-J, and you can order that document for a small fee from the address printed on the back of this card. Once you have obtained the document, and attended an orientation and been certified in an official training session, you will be able to offer your other guests delicious AMSB 01-3382-Sausage-Js, and I think this will do a lot for your business. It may improve the clientele. The AMSB document specifies a list of acceptable meats, including pork shank, smoked carp, textured jerboa protein, Michigan Mock Steak, turkey-pork shoulder, and various others. I'll let you surprise me. I would like two and one-half of these sausages, roasted over hot coals. I'm sure you know what I mean when I say "hot coals," don't you?

A breakfast such as I am specifying would be useless without home-fried potatoes. Because my own home is far away across the ocean, I think it will be acceptable if you fry the potatoes in the home of my Aunt. I have been staying with her this week. She lives only a mile from here, and her kitchen, though small, is quaint and PH-neutral. Her name is Edna. She will demand to know all about you, of course, especially your romantic life. Edna is a very lonely old woman. But you must tell her nothing. She will want to assist you in the home-frying of the potatoes, but don't let her. She is not a professional, like you. I have laid aside four potatoes for home-frying, they are in a sealed cryogenic container in a briefcase wrapped in plastic in the cold-storage freezer in the sub-basement of Aunt Edna's house. It's very dark down there, and there are a lot of things to bump into. You can locate the cold-storage freezer by its telltale sickly buzz-hum. There's no light inside the freezer either, but the briefcase is to the left, wrapped in plastic. I have no idea what those other things are in there, and I certainly don't want them introduced into my potatoes. Simply boil the potatoes for fourteen minutes or until they become softer than a soft apple but not quite as soft as a hard pear, then chop them in whatever manner you prefer — I'm not picky — before home-frying them on a PH-neutral cooking surface oiled with walnut oil and heated to 260 degrees Celsius. When they are done home-frying, season them and rush them hither.

Toast is futile. It would take too long to describe what I really want, and I'm getting hungry, so let's just forget about the toast. Just bring me 300 milliliters of boiling water, thirty grams of raw coffee beans, a Bunsen burner, a piece of silk, a machete and six inches of string while I'm waiting. And a cloth napkin, please. Thank you. ☜

Poor Ivan Is In Love

Our poor friend Ivan has fallen in most unfortunate
and inadvisable love — with a girl, no less. We saw
him today, beside the Bottle-Cap Factory that graces
our industrial skyline. We wore the tweed coat and
chambray trousers that are the unofficial uniform of
our Group. But Ivan, he arrived draped in a long
white clinical jacket, toying with a dilapidated
stethoscope as if unsure of its function.

"She's interested in Medicine," he confessed, and
blew his nose on a crumpled paper shoe of the hospital
variety. "I've been reading on the subject myself, just
browsing really, but it astounds me what can be
accomplished in our age with ... you know, sick
people."

"Ivan," we chided in our firm but affectionate tone,
"we are meeting tomorrow at the Library to analyze
One Hundred Years of Solitude. May one presume
one's attendance?"

Ivan weighed the brass and rubber stethoscope in
his left hand, the tissue shoe in his right, perhaps
deciding which would make the more impressive
bouquet. Inside the factory, able and responsible
bottle-capiers hammered and twisted at their work.
Poor Ivan!

◉　　◉　　◉

Poor, foolish Ivan. We saw him again today, outside
the gates that encircle the manicured grounds of the
Advertising Building, button on the epaulet of out
industrial skyline. We wore the deep blue necktie that
is the secret identifier of the members of our Group.

But Ivan, deluded boy (clever though he may be in the nobler disciplines), wore a paint-spattered T-shirt and comfortable jeans. He quite reeked of turpentine, and his hands and arms were streaked in orange and cobalt.

"She's fond of art," he apologized.

"Multifaceted, your Juliet."

"I must apologize that I missed last night's discussion. I'm afraid I was absorbed in my experiments with texture. At any rate, how did it go?"

"Go? Where would it have gone? Did you expect me to talk to myself for two hours? In the Library?"

He examined his shoe. "Sorry," he sighed.

"And your intaglio," we probed, "how did it 'go'?"

"Quite smoothly, I'm afraid." He paused, clearly dejected. "But concurrently, I'm finding the process itself, the experience of the failure to paint, it's enticing. I've already failed several portraits, though when faced with certain beauty, the oil and brush simply ... reaffirm a certain ... exquisite ..." At this his eyes achieved an abstract-expressionistic quality. We took notice of a number, possibly a telephone number, smeared on the length on his left arm.

"Well," we commented, "the visual arts certainly have their place in our industrial skyline, when executed by the visualists themselves. But please, Ivan, members of our Group are scheduled to meet tomorrow morning at the University to recruit new members. Without you we should be deluged."

Ivan knelt and studied the texture of the sidewalk with semi-professional interest. Inside the great gray Advertising Building, persuasive new arguments bubbled in their flasks, awaiting mass release.

"I'll be there, of course," he said, and started away.

"And Ivan?"

"Hm?"

"Tomorrow evening at the Library, the membership will discuss Paradise Lost."

⊙   ⊙   ⊙

We met that morning at the wide steps of the University, erudite spire jutting from the belly of our industrial skyline. I wore the long tan mackintosh and gray fedora that is the official uniform of our Group, when it's raining. Ivan brought a duck, in a wire and wooden cage. I pointedly ignored this duck.

Ivan collected signatures while I addressed the throng:

"JOIN THE GREAT BOOKS DISCUSSION GROUP!"

"DISCUSS ... GREAT BOOKS!"

"MEET INTELLECTUALS!"

"UNVEIL NEW HORIZONS OF EXPERIENCE!"

"IMPROVE YOUR STUDY SKILLS!"

But the throng was distracted. They hurried up and down the wide steps, rushing to warmth indoors or to waiting autos, a few pausing to examine the shivering duck, but then continuing on. By noon, Ivan's few collected signatures had been dissolved into his soaked and limp legal pad by the rain. I sat beside him, and glared at the duck. He hesitated.

"She likes —"

"Ivan!" I shrieked. "What's wrong with you? You were once so dependable! So articulate! Great books spilled out their truths at your interrogation. Libraries wept!"

Ivan gazed into the deep brown eyes of the cold, cold duck.

"Look at you now! Fickle as the publishers of the Tolstoy Quarterly! More faddish that the deconstructionists of Joyce! Your mind is turning to effluvium over that girl. She's no good for you."

"I'm not coming tonight."

"The Group is adrift without you, Ivan."

"I can't apologize enough, I know. Tomorrow night I give my word I will attend. But tonight ..." At this he gathered up his duck cage in his spindly arms and smirked. "... I have a date."

One sensed, from within the University, a great many tests being simultaneously failed.

◉   ◉   ◉

That evening our Group convened at the Library, vast collective memory of our industrial skyline. I wore the powdered wig and coke-bottle bifocals that are *de rigueur* for such formal situations.

At that meeting, a motion was put forth calling for Ivan's expulsion from the Group, on the grounds of his recent lack of dedication and sharply declined attendance.

A lively debate ensued. Attention was drawn to Ivan's distinguished record of achievement, his seniority, and the questionable validity of the fifty percent quorum. Personal loyalties were also drawn into play. The motion was eventually rescheduled for

the next meeting, when we planned to discuss Dante's
Inferno.

◉   ◉   ◉

The following dusk I found him at the graveyard, that
plot where we deposit the casualties of our industrial
skyline. He wandered slowly from headstone to
headstone, a loose hemp noose dangling from his neck
and trailing through the flowers behind him. His arms
hung lifeless. His head hung low. His shoulder pack
flopped against his hip with each ragged step.

"Fond of death is she, Ivan?"

He submitted to brief, morose laughter, which
devolved to a profound shudder. "Actually," he
croaked, "she has a boyfriend. A chemical engineer,
who yachts. She's told me all about him, last night
over cabernet and blackened duck."

We blanched. "Ivan ... you didn't?"

"I meant to impress her with my multifacilities.
However ..." and he sank back into miasma.

We sat there for some time without talking. We
had never seen our friend Ivan so devoid of
enthusiasm.

"Why," he asked, "is so much of our great literature
concerned with romantic failure? Why do stories of
success and suitable endings appear so transparent to
us? What is the attraction of tragedy?"

"The attraction of tragedy in literature," I replied,
"is that it happens to others."

We sat there for some time more, still not talking.
It began to rain.

"Ivan?"

"Hm?"

"Did you really slaughter that duck?"

"I did."

"The Greeks, you know, and the Romans —"

"Auguries, yes. I thought of that as well."

"Well then, did the entrails of the duck, did they, um, portend anything to you?"

He giggled, and scratched his chin. "To me they foretold unlucky times ahead — for the duck." At this I chuckled. "And," he added, "that butchering should be left to butchers. When I slit the poor creature's belly, all the while thinking 'You are a great sacrifice to my love, noble bird,' the guts that spilled out were the most unromantic thing I have beheld since my Biology dissections. I meant to prepare Orange Duck, you know."

"Ambitious."

"Yes, well, hubris had quite overtaken me. Blackened Duck was an inspiration attributable more to an overfed hibachi than to me. Nevertheless, I felt the sauce sustained the dish. I copied it from a crumbling old edition of Rombauer, which I found at a bookstore that just opened near the Styrofoam Decomposition Facility — you know, that inflatable building that gets smaller on weekends?"

"Yes, I know the one. Right beside the Darts Academy."

"Directly across from there, where previously there was a tap dancing studio — forced out by the neighbors, I was told — now sits an antiquarian bookseller's, operated by the most bizarre little man.

You must meet him. He knows from Goethe."

"That's exciting, Ivan. Shall we go there now?"

"I could accompany you in less than half an hour, if you would wait while I finish this errand." He doffed the shoulder pack, and from it withdrew a garden spade, a small ornate crucifix, and a Tupperware box. Inside the translucent plastic box I could see the charred remains of some meal, garnished with a few carrots. "I feel I've done this creature an injustice, you see." And, choosing a spot a few yards from us, he began to dig.

Poor Ivan. He is incurably romantic. ✒

Class Action Application

ABSTRACT: Consideration as Plaintiff in Court Case
US-783471.913 Class-Action: (Plaintiffs) vs. Dow
Corning Manufacturers, Prosthetics & Medical
Implements (aka "Dow Corning Breast-Implant
Class-Action Suit")

CONSIDERATION PREPARED BY:
> Mykle Hansen, freelance lawyer

NAME OF CONSIDERANT:
> Clay Connaly

AGE OF CONSIDERANT:
> 31

DATE OF BREAST IMPLANT PROCEDURE:
> January 3, 1995

LOCATION (FACILITY, STATE) OF BREAST
IMPLANT PROCEDURE:
> St. Francis Church of Christ Hospital, TX

PURPOSE OF BREAST IMPLANT PROCEDURE
(COSMETIC, RECONSTRUCTIVE, OTHER):
> N/A (see exposition)

DAMAGES SOUGHT BY CONSIDERANT:
> Fifteen Million, Four Thousand Fifty Seven
Dollars ($15,004,057)

INTRODUCTION OF CONSIDERANT:
Clay Connaly ("Client") is a 31 year-old male. Client
was employed by St. Francis Church of Christ
Hospital, Loredo, TX between August of 1984 and
June of 1986 in the capacity of Nursing Assistant
("NA"). (Employment terminated satisfactorily — see
disposition of Church of Christ Hospital Nursing Staff

Manager June Cleary, attached.) During this period, Client obtained a "Stealth-Sheen" Dow Corning manufactured artificial breast implant ("artificial breast").

DESCRIPTION OF INITIAL BREAST IMPLANT PROCEDURE:
Artificial breast had become un-sterilized during routine medical practices on Jan 3, 1985. Specifically, a Church of Christ Hospital cosmetic surgery patient had objected to insufficient volume of artificial breast immediately before surgery, requiring surgeon to move to a larger size. Smaller-sized artificial breast, unsterile, was given by surgeon to Client with instructions to "dispose of (it) in proper manner". Client disposed of artificial breast in his home, specifically upon 1860's-era mission-style coffee table ("table") in downstairs front guest-reception area, utilization characterized by Client as "conversation piece". This arrangement was considered "proper manner" by Client and constituted faithful execution of instructions and performance of NA duties. Furthermore, it kept with Client's laudable ongoing efforts to reduce waste and encourage environmentally-friendly practices at Church of Christ Hospital.

DESCRIPTION OF COMPLICATIONS/TRAUMA:
Artificial breast remained stable in client's downstairs front guest-reception area for several years, beyond Client's period of employment with Church of Christ Hospital, until date of artificial breast failure: Nov. 23, 1988, under following circumstances:

Client held a pre-Thanksgiving semi-public open house event ("shindig") in his home, wherein guests became interested in the entertainment potential of artificial breast as party favor. At one point, normal squeezing/groping/fondling of artificial breast — said squeezing/groping/fondling well within design tolerances for this Dow product, and we must note Dow advertising/promotional information sent to doctors in 1983-1984 (see attachment) included photographs of off-duty medical professionals employing similar artificial implant products in similar educational/entertainment capacities, thereby DEMONSTRATING AN INTENDED USE OF THE PRODUCT — said squeezing of Dow artificial breast implant caused implant to burst, traumatically.

INITIAL ASSESSMENT OF DAMAGES DUE TO COMPLICATIONS/TRAUMA:

1) Artificial breast liquid silicone core caused indelible stains, damage to table. Replacement cost assessed in 1979 at $750, adjusted to current dollars at $2127.

2) Liquid silicone core caused indelible stains, damage to Persian rug. Replacement cost estimated at $1200 in 1988, adjusted to $1755.

3) Liquid silicone core caused indelible stains, damage to personal items & clothing of several shindig participants. Client reimbursed participants with complimentary beverages valued at $120 in 1988, adjusted to $175.

4) Damage to Client's standing in the community as a result of public artificial breast failure is significant, but difficult to quantify. We note this for purposes of arbitration only.

5) Trauma, embarrassment from the artificial breast failure/bursting event left Client with a lingering fear and distrust of artificial breasts (see attached deposition of Dr. Lawrence Fokker, Ph.D, psychiatric consultant to Client). This phobia has significantly hampered the progress of Client's career in the film industry. Although Client has bravely battled this problem and met with some career success, he has done so though the abandonment of a path towards feature film directing, which his breast-failure-induced phobic trauma makes impossibly difficult for him. Instead Client has channeled his strength and creativity into the field of computer animation. (Attached disposition by Dr. Fokker explains this "replacement-anxiety strategy" as pathological and involuntary.) The net result is a significant, irreversible diminution of Client's earning power and capacity for joy. It is impossible to know just how high Client may have risen in the field of feature film directing had this terrible trauma not wounded his psyche. Our figure of fifteen million dollars is based on our estimate of only the last ten years' lost potential, and does not come close to fully reimbursing him for the damage to his future potential. 👁

I Called Your Dream

How did you sleep last night? Did you dream
anything? Me too. Did you dream about a long
hallway? A boat? A telephone? Did the telephone
ring? Did you answer the telephone? Why not? I
dreamed I called you last night, and you didn't answer.
Why didn't you answer when I called? Yes, I know you
were asleep, I was asleep too. I called your dream from
my dream. How? I asked the operator. Umm ... a
black woman I think, sounded like she was about my
age or a bit younger. Very helpful and courteous. I
don't remember the number, but I wrote it down on
the telephone book in my dream. Umm ... I think she
said she was with US West. Yeah, they're everywhere.
But maybe you get to have GTE in your dreams.
You'd know if you ever picked up the phone. Yes, I
know we call each other all the time. Okay, I call you
all the time, sure. It's fun! I thought, hey, I'm
dreaming, I wonder if this phone works. It's like when
I got my cell phone and I called you from all those
places? Hey, I'm on a bus! Hey, I'm in an elevator!
Hey, I'm in my own hall closet! You know, it was fun.
I figured, what if I can call up Nancy in her dreams
from my dreams. I bet it would have worked! How? I
don't know how, I don't even know how my cell phone
works. It uses waves. Anyway you can do anything in
dreams, that's the whole point. I read that somewhere.
Anyway I didn't mean to disturb you or interrupt
anything. Why, what were you doing when the phone
rang? Why not? Just curious, geez. I'll tell you what I
... yeah, I was um ... in this office, in a really tall
building downtown, only it had only stairs, no elevator
or escalator, and I worked on the 37th floor, I

remember that, it was a temp job that the agency placed me with and I had to get there at exactly midnight and start working, but everybody else was there too, I remember it was very important stuff they did in the legal profession and they all worked 24 hours a day. I made copies. I had to use this photocopier that was on the 34th floor, three floors down from where my cube was, so I had to keep going out into this big stairwell where the stairs didn't have any railings, and I'd look down this mile-deep stairwell at all the people going up and down, and there'd be big groups of people very precariously trying to squeeze past other big groups of people traveling in the other direction, not passing single-file which would have been the safest way, but instead shoving straight through each other, and I remember watching someone fall from a ledge above me, and the first time I came back from using the copier ... the copier itself had this computer in it, and these big seizing arms, and the copier would work okay if it was left unplugged, but if someone plugged it in it would wake up and get evil. The seizing arms jumped out and yanked my copy jobs away from me and threw the papers into this metal box in its side than sprung open, kind of an iron-lidded incinerator-style box, the copier was also apparently part of the central heating system of this huge building, and I remember it was part of some futuristic head-management environmental control system that was a big cost-saving feature of this brand-new futuristic office building. When the copier finished my copy job (fifteen copies stapled and collated) they came out on this other extendo-robotic arm with a weird cat-litter scoop attachment on the end, I mean, yeah, I mean it had dried bits of cat litter on it and it smelled like serious cat butt, and there were my copies in this little dirty scoop. So I'm all, okay, I grab the copies but the other extendo-robotic arm, the one with the grasping pincer on the end, it has a longer reach and it's sort of hovering above the cat-litter scoop, grasping pincer wide open, and it looks like it wants to grab me and copy me. So I say to this copier, Where's My Originals, and the copier laughs — it's got this little blue screen way on the other end of the room with a little graphical user interface on it, and little individual windows pop up, and each one just says HA! in big type, and they pop up one at a time, HA! HA! HA! HA!, and the extendo-robotic arms jiggle with laughter, super creepy. But while it's laughing I grab the copies out of its scoop and run out the door, and then I'm back on the staircase only I notice that very very slowly, the staircase, the one with no railing, has been retracting into the walls, so that where it was like three people wide before, winding around this incredibly long 100-story shaft, now it's like one and seven-eighths people wide, and I head on upwards, and as I do I pass people heading downwards, and they all want me to pass them on the right, which is the outside, you know, the edge of the stairs is there and there's occasionally people in suits — everybody wears either suits with leather shoes or like jogging outfits with huge Nikes, Nikes the size of ski boots, and these Nikes are like specially designed for traction and agility when climbing treacherous staircases, and the people who have the Nikes on have an automatic advantage in any of these climbing situations, and that's when I realize that I'm wearing only my underwear, and this pair of little fuzzy duck slippers, slippers that are shaped like ducks — and there's occasionally people in suits falling, from above, on down towards the bottom of the stair shaft, and they don't scream or say anything, they just plummet on down and you never hear them hit. None of the guys with the jogging suits have fallen yet at that point, although you can see how even they eventually would. So I'm passing people on the right, where they get to cling to the wall and I have to go around them, and it's not impossible to do, it's not like they're going to exactly push me, but they all seem kind of pissed-off and offended and irritated that when I pass them I stand so close, invading their personal space when I'm passing them, and I touch one guy accidentally and he sort of shoves me as I pass him and I freak out and almost lose my balance, but I don't. And I can tell that the stairs are still retracting, and the funny thing is that I remember that this particular super-modern office building is designed with Self-Cleaning Stairs, and that there's all these signs above all the doors that say to Stay Out Of The Stairwell During The Cleaning Cycle, but when the copying job fell in my IN box on my desk in my cube, I forgot to check the clock ... anyway I have to finally pass one of these big phalanxes of like ten guys in Nikes and jogging suits, the suits are all the same color, red, with stripes down the sleeves and legs and with high collars held tight with two metal snaps on each neck, they're jogging down the steps in single file, and they come towards me and yell

"Stand to the right!" but there's no room, so I turn around and run back downwards aways until I get to the base of the 36th floor, and I duck in the door there, just moments before these joggers shove me into the abyss. But in there ... well, that part's weird, but after a while I get out again and ... no, well, it's kind of sexual, that's all. Well, no, it's gross. No really. You don't want to hear about that stuff. I'm boring you, aren't I? Really? Okay ... well, stop me when it gets too gross for you then, but I open this door and inside there's this long wood-paneled hallway, with rows of flowers on either side of the hallway, it's like a very fancy reception area, and I go up to the desk at the end and it's this receptionist who's got like no clothes on, at all, just one of those phone headsets. Yeah and ... no, I didn't "do" her! Shut up! I'm so sure! No, I just said ... I'm telling you, okay, just listen, so I'm all, ahem, Hello there miss, I was just dropping by to get out of the Stairway Cleaning Cycle, and she smiles, and she's all Oh yeah, the Cleaning Cycle, I hate that, isn't it a drag? Feel free to wait here in our waiting area as long as you like. Can I get you some Maxwell House International Blend? We have Irish Cream, Italian Zest, Swedish Romp, etc, etc? And I'm like, Well, thanks very much ma'am but I've got this very important photocopying job I've just got to get back to the head office upstairs, and do you know if there's any way at all that I can get up there while the stairwell is closed? And she goes Welllll, and then she looks around, and then she whispers to me, There's an executive elevator that we're not supposed to use, but I know the combination, come around here, and then she ducks under her desk, and I wait for her to sit back up, but she doesn't, and when I look around behind her desk I see there's a little door down there, and when I crawl through the door I'm in a tiny, tiny room, and she's there too, and she's still naked and I'm still in my underwear ... and she presses the number 37 on the wall, and there's a ding, and then I climb out the door and I'm in my office again. So I go back to my desk, and ... no, I don't remember where she went. She stayed in the elevator. I went back to my desk, but when I got there there was this note on my chair that said CHARLIE! CHECK YOUR VOICE MAIL! but I didn't have a phone in my cube, and there wasn't one on the whole floor, and then I remembered, there's a pay phone in the stairwell. So I stuck my head out into the self-cleaning stairwell one more time, just opened the door and looked out there, and what I saw was the stairs had retracted back to about six inches, and for several floors above and below there were these guys in jogging suits with enormous shoes who were standing on the remaining edge of stairway, backs to the wall, shuffling slowly sideways either up or down the staircase, and I watched as two of them approached each other going opposite ways, and they did this sort of acrobatic maneuver where one of them would spin around on one inside toe so that suddenly he was face to face and sort of ... sort of embracing the other one, and then he'd flip over again, spinning on his other toe, so that he was against the wall and that way the two of them would have passed each other. And they all seemed to be pretty good at this, and without getting huffy with each other either, and I could tell that the stairs were almost retracted and still slowly retracting, but down the stairs to my right only about ten feet away was this pay telephone. So I figured, well, I have to check my voice mail, it's only ten feet, it'll be a quick call, the ledge is retracting pretty slowly ... yeah, well, it's a dream. Don't you do dumb things in your dreams? I'm always having ... I'm always about to have unprotected intercourse with total strangers in my dreams, that's pretty dumb. With ... lots of people. Why? People I don't know sometimes. Well yeah of course it's all harmless, it's a dream, so like quit interRUPting me oKAY? I'm so sure. Anyway: I slide down this ledge with my back to the wall, and it's slow going but I reach the phone, and I get change out of my pocket and put it in the phone but then I realize I don't know what the voice mail number is. So then, that was when, specifically, I called ... you! First I called 411, got your number from the operator from US West ... sure I have it memorized, but in the dream I didn't, but I wrote it down on the cover of the phone book, 553-0861. And then ... what do you mean what happened, bitch? Well, did you answer the frickin' phone last night or what? Did you? No you did NOT! So it just rang and rang, and I redialed 'cause I thought maybe I dialed it wrong but it just rang some more, and I felt the ledge going out from under my heels so I was just standing on my toes, and hanging onto the phone book that's like hanging from that little length of cable. Like I knew I had to get off the ledge but I didn't want to let go of the phone, right? And then I slipped, and I hung there by the telephone handset and the phone book ... and then the alarm went off. Well, not exactly scary ... most of my dreams are like that. I didn't wake up in a sweat or anything. Why, what are your dreams like?

Welcome to Springfield, Mass —
Home of Absorbine Jr.!

So this is where Absorbine Jr. lives, along with old Mister Absorbine Sr. in their massive research chalet in downtown Springfield, Mass.

"We like it fine," said the limber-jointed patriarch as he showed me past the long cases that hold his antique bottle collection. "We could live anywhere in town, of course, but here we're closer to the heart of things. My son says he has to be near the lab at all times, in the event of a sudden brainstorm, you know. Come, we'll see if he's there."

Soon enough we came to a wide atrium, thick with the activities of two dozen sprightly septuagenarian lab assistants and well-furnished with racks and benches of glass pipettes, flasks, inhalators, and other chemist's equipment. Junior (as we learned he is called even by his many subordinates) wasted no time with introductions, instead beckoning that our party should hurry to observe through his well-oiled microscope a drama unfolding at the cellular front.

"This will fascinate you," the young inventor explained in boyish tones. "Dyed blue, and more to the right, you'll see — here, I'll adjust the lens — you'll see a strain of the E. Coli bacterium that has been nurtured in a distillate of my famous namesake balm. Dyed red, and huddled on the left edge ... here!" He gestured with the tip of a pen as we attempted to maintain focus — "here is a colony of E. Coli bred in a dish of that nefarious autotoxin sold to the public as DMSO. You have no doubt heard the health and rejuvenative claims made for this stuff by an assortment of untrained chemists, country doctors and, ahem, herbalists. Now watch closely."

We did as the good doctor bade — for we do not recall if he holds an accredited Doctorate, but he seems on first encounter eminently worthy of the title — and we watched as, on the hair's-width field of microscopic battle, the red and blue cells engaged in mortal combat *cilium a cilium.* As predicted, it was a rout. "I have staged many such experiments, and the results are uniform. I hope that when my aggregate findings are published in the Dermatic Events Monitor, an informed public will become less credulous of such swindlement."

While he conducted us on a topical tour of lab activities — an array of research and development projects too exhaustive to enumerate — we asked him how he came to the world of applied topiary theory. "My old Dad was the one who brought me my first jar of cold cream, back when I was a youngster. I used to race bicycles in those days, and I knew a lot of other racers, amateurs and professionals, who suffered from joint soreness. But at the time I was more concerned with keeping my hubs and chains lubricated, and dealing with the chafing and cracking, in certain sensitive areas, that are the mascots of professional racers and dedicated tourists alike. One day Pa suggested I try the cold creme for my chapped areas, and on that occasion I was by chance out of axle grease, having used it up not just on the axle bearings

but also on my chain and derailleurs ... I'm afraid I've never been able to put things where they belong.
"At any rate, I experimented with the cream, found it useful in a number of areas, and yet lacking in all of them. I wondered if I might gain added penetration by adding menthol; whether beeswax or paraffin might improve bonding, and so on. The formal study of chemistry came later, but it was there in my father's shack —"

Suddenly the great man's reminiscences were fissured by a deafening blast from the far side of the hall. For a moment panic reigned amid the burning smells and flying glass. A fire alarm rang out as flames spread rapidly across tables and floors. A coughing older gentleman found us cover behind a nearby chemical vat as Junior, clearly a man of action, raced up the catwalk and opened the valves of an elaborate system of pipes and tubing that laced the ceiling. "Stay calm, everybody!" he bellowed, and with the twist of a final giant knob the room began to fill with a thick, creamy, aromatic rain. The flames, which seconds earlier had threatened to engulf us, were quickly extinguished, and the unpleasant acid smells were replaced with a cool eucalyptus flavour. The good doctor closed the hydraulic system and climbed carefully back down the hot, stiff and well-lubricated iron rungs.
He winked. "Absorbine Jr. — just the thing for chemical fires! But gracious, your suit is coated ... please, let one of my assistants escort you to the baths and attend to your needs."

And he made good on that promise. After we paid a relaxing visit to the laboratory showers and sauna, our clothes were returned to us, dry and perfectly clean, with only a pleasantly lingering odor to remind us of the amusing episode. We later learned that they had undergone an experimental, but totally successful, chemical dry-cleaning method developed by Absorbine and his staff, and employing again his signature cream. Indeed, we marveled, if there are no panaceas, this is yet the closest thing.

We concluded our visit after a tour of the immaculately kept yards, the freshly-scented stables, and the gymnasium and bicycle track that receive much of Junior's leisure attention, and which he egalitariastically shares with his remarkably muscular and flexible staff of older scientists. It is all as fabulous as you have heard, and befitting this man, who has given so much to his community and the world with his brilliant innovations. We left convinced of the exciting future which Science holds for us all, and of the bounteous wealth and glistening goodness of human Genius. Truly, there is no better time than now to be alive. &

Enough About Me

But enough about me. Tell me about you. The real you. Be honest. So, you're an investment analyst? Sounds interesting. Are you rich? Ha ha, just kidding, no, seriously, are you rich? How rich are you? What kind of car do you drive? Is it imported? How fast does it go? Is there a cup holder? Is it one of the retractable kind of ones? really? wow. So what does an investment analyst do? uh huh? uh huh? mmm. interesting. So, what kind of movies to you like? Do you like the ones with lots of special effects? The ones with Gwyneth Paltrow in them? The ones where stuff explodes? Did you see Titanic? really? Me too! wow. Do you like the ones where they're all from some foreign country and there's little words at the bottom of the screen and you can't figure out what's going on and they're really really long? oh. really? oh. So, do you like sports? What kind of sports? Do you like football or baseball? Do you like hockey? Do you like Wayne Gretsky? Not personally, I mean. Do you know Wayne Gretsky? Personally? Wow. No, me neither. Do you like wrestling? Do you like the World's Strongest Man competitions on ESPN2? Uh huh? Where they have to pull trucks uphill with their teeth and then catch kegs of beer that are dropped off a diving platform, and then lift farm animals over their heads? Really? Wow. How about water ballet? hmm. So. Tell me about your family. Are you an only child? Brothers or sisters? Sisters? How many sisters? Really? Wow. That's a lot of sisters. Do they all look like you? How old is the oldest one? What's the difference between the oldest one's age and your age, in years, approximately? Oh, I don't know, just curious.

So, do you read books? Hmm. Do you read
magazines? Which ones? Do you read Time? Do you
read People? Do you read TV Guide? Do you watch a
lot of TV? Really? Wow. What shows do you watch?
Do you watch Ellen? Really? No, I've never seen it
myself actually. Yeah. No. Yeah. But I heard it's
really really good. Do you worry about the future?
Really? Do you worry about the millennium? What
do you think's going to happen? Floods? Famine?
Computer crisis? really? Do you think it's going to
last? wow. really? How does this affect your job as an
investment analyst? Hmm. What about global
warming? What do you think about population
increase? Really? Wow. Yeah, me too, someday. You
know, when I find the right person. Did you like the
meal? How's the wine? Did you fart? Really? hmm.
no, it wasn't me. Do you want desert? A cordial? A
drink someplace? My place? Really? Wow. You
know, you're really interesting. No, really. 👁

The New 1999 Jeep Interloper!

Pelted by snow, by sleet, by rain. Pelted by stones, by fish, by golf balls the size of golf balls. They slam into the roof of the car. Pelted by bricks, little chunks of them fly off, they are kiln-fired bricks with the name of the kiln that fired them stamped on the side. They bang the car like a big steel drum, but with the AEDS (Anti-Environmental Dampening System) we hardly notice. Bob cranks up the car stereo. The subwoofer thunders as we are pelted some more, by hot iron chains, by flaming spears. They bounce right off the impact-resistant windshield, although they do mar the top layer of Combat-Formulated Turtle Wax. Now we are pelted by actual cats and dogs. They are not happy about pelting us. We roll on over them, crushing their whimpering bodies. It's surprisingly comfortable, riding in Bob's brand-new 1999 Jeep Interloper with all the options.

We are on the Black Island of Tartulia, in the South Pacific, climbing the Forbidden Path up the Volcano of Certain Smiting. The volcano doesn't want us here, but Bob assures me that his new sport-utility vehicle is more than a match for any third-rate speed-bump of an island deity. The guy at the dealership gave his personal guarantee, says Bob. We scour along over the debris and broken meat and sharp volcanic stone, winding up the evil road. Bob hits the shuffle button on the trunk-mounted shock-resistant one-hundred disc CD changer. We listen to the Sugarcubes as we're pelted with blades, with huge boulders, with flaming tires. Bob activates the four-wheel drive.

Bob is my team-leader's co-supervisor's co-supervisor at work. Neither of us are sure whether or not that makes him one of my direct bosses, but he is a vice president of some kind and I am not. Among the stratospheres of management, he is the ozone layer, and I am fog. We were sent out here as ethics-assessment visitors to one of our assembly plants on the other side of the island. Bob organized the trip and got approval and funding from the board. I volunteered to accompany him as video camera operator because I figured it'd be a fairly easy way to do something ethical for Third-World workers, which was my New Years' resolution. Bob says we'll drop by the factory later, after we break in his new car.

We round the ragged east side of the volcano's slope and approach a great stone gate, carved with mythic runes of anti-invitation. Guarding the gate are a pair of three-headed hellhounds, snarling, spitting sulphur, black skinned, red eyed, their barks hollow and enormous. Bob switches the CD to Metallica, rolls up the windows and locks the doors with an automatic pop. The dogs scream. Bob honks at them. They howl. He honks. One dog growls and leaps forward, covering the distance between us in one leap, and its huge snout bangs against the windshield, and its red flaming eyes bore into our souls. Bob activates the windshield washers and sprays the hound with ammonia-based window cleaner. The other dog has gotten behind us, it's chewing on one of our wheels, I can feel the suspension compensating. The anti-theft system is triggered. The dogs howl and bark and the car goes beep beep beep beep whoooop whooooop rrt rrt rrt rrt ooo eee ooo eee arp arp arp arp arp. The frontmost dog tears at the antenna with its powerful jaws. A mechanized voice demands: STEP AWAY FROM THE VEHICLE! THIS CAR IS PROTECTED BY AN AUTOMATED SECURITY SYSTEM! The front dog climbs onto the roof and claws viciously at the bike racks. Seeing an opening, Bob hits the gas and races ahead through the gates, scattering the dogs behind him, the car still shouting ARMED RESPONSE! ARMED RESPONSE! as we speed away up the steep incline, spitting volcanic gravel behind us.

Bob is pleased with his victory, but expresses concern about the antenna, which is an expensive part, as are all of the other parts on his new seventy-three-thousand dollar all-terrain luxury adventure system. The rear left end of the car lolls a bit. Bob says we have a flat ... but don't worry, the tires will patch themselves and reinflate automatically. They're German. As the tire rejuvenates, we are pelted by human heads. Dismembered, screaming heads, and what they're screaming is largely non-constructive. The self-reinflating tire has reinflated itself and announces this fact with a synthesized strain from Beethoven's Fifth. It is indeed a tough and fearless car, but despite the luxurious leather bucket seats and the gyrostabilizing cup-holders I still can't quite relax. Now beheaded bodies are plummeting from above. One presumes these are the bodies the heads came from. They're quite large and all over the place, and one of them lands smack-dab on the hood and claws and writhes, and mimes something unholy, and Bob brakes, to jerk it off the hood, and then accelerates, to roll on over it, as if it were a fallen branch or a traffic cone. And while he's doing that he talks on and on about the great suffering he's endured: the shopping, the feature-comparing and the price-comparing, the test-driving, the different selling points of the cars he almost bought but didn't, the lying salesmen, and then how the self-reinflating tires were very expensive and he almost didn't get them, but then again look how they've already paid for themselves. Meanwhile a dismembered hand has grabbed the left-side mirror and is maliciously maladjusting it as we continue through the bloody carnage.

We round another sharp turn. We are very near the summit now, behind the shadow of the volcanic cone, and the pelting has suddenly ceased. The sky has gone flat, and the ambient temperature, according to the dashboard climactic comparator, is stifling. Inside the car it's a cool 70 degrees Fahrenheit, 30% humidity. The terrain through which we're moving is all black, sooty volcanic coral and hardened patches of smooth black lava, and sulphurous steam rises from vents all around us. Bob switches the air system to "recirculate", dials in a pine-fresh scent, turns on the fog lights and the running lights and we continue on.

We turn another corner and there ahead of us is the final barrier, and it's a doozy: a long straight corridor between two high volcanic berms, crisscrossed with rows and rows of those severe tire damage spiky things, the kind they have in Los Angeles parking lots, which retract harmlessly into the ground when you drive over them the right way, but which punch giant inch-wide holes in your steel belts when you drive over them the wrong way, and the wrong way is the way we're going. There's thirteen tiers of them between us and what looks like the very last turn.

Bob puts it in park. He's thinking. He didn't know they had those things in the South Pacific. He was expecting, maybe, bamboo. He gets out to have a closer look, and I follow him. I kneel to examine the first row of teeth — it's razor sharp and well-oiled and when I try to touch it, it snaps at me. But I hop over it easily enough. By all appearances we're less than 100 yards from the top, and I suggest to Bob that we just walk the rest of the way. He looks at me with disgust. What about the beer, he says. What about the folding chairs and stuff, our picnic, all of it is in the back of the car and Bob doesn't feel like shlepping it all up some hill. It's been a long drive. He curses, and kicks a stone at the battalion of blades. They snicker and snap.

We get back in the car. Bob says nothing for a moment, then puts it in Reverse, then checks his left-side mirror and sees that it's maladjusted. He tries to aim it with the servo joystick mirror aimer thing but it's not responding. He curses. He rests his lower lip on the steering wheel and squints.

Bob switches out of Reverse and into Low, leans on the horn and rages full-ahead. We gain speed quickly and cross the first row of spikes doing almost forty. The car bounces, and we cross the second row, still gaining speed, and the car jumps, there's a double-popping sound and it kneels, and then the third and fourth bumps we almost feel through the positraction independent suspension and self-compensating hydraulic shocks. The fifth row is softer, the hiss of air escaping from little holes grows louder and the rumble of the air compressor shifts up in pitch as it struggles to reinflate the tires. But it's not working so well, and when we cross the sixth row the car kneels again, and on the seventh row it kneels some more, we're no longer accelerating, reflected in the passenger-side mirror I see shredded pieces of former tire flying out behind us, looking limp and defeated and German, we're losing our momentum, rolling on the rims, and the rims are scraping on the rocks and knives as we cross the eighth, ninth, tenth, eleventh rows on pure momentum, slowing down, unable to get any purchase, sparks and rocks spitting from below us, and Bob stops and starts, stops and starts, rocking the car forward like you would rock some cheap two-wheel drive car stuck in a mudhole, we scramble over the twelfth barrier this way, ride up against the thirteenth ... scrape against it with the front wheels, which Bob twists to the left and right (effortlessly, due to the power-assisted steering) ... and just when all seems lost, something hooks to one of the wheels and we are launched powerfully forward, across the last row of tire-eating blades, and up along the flattening incline we scramble, and around the last corner, and there, at the other side of a clearing, is the edge of the volcano.

Bob gets out. I get out. It's silent, the sky is now a dingy red, there's no sensation of heat or cold, only space and silence. The volcano makes a low quiet sound like an immense old lung slowly inhaling. Bob pulls his HandiCam out of the trunk, points it at me and says "All right, we made it! Let's say Hi to the folks back home!" 👁

Trans-Continental Fiber Tunnel
Installation Notification Notice

US West Communications Customer:
Martha Q. Customer
1887 Solemn Upswing Grade
Portland, OR 97221

September 9, 1999

Dear Customer Customer:

In order to serve you better, US West is undertaking an
exciting new expansion of our service offerings. One
important aspect of this expansion is the new
Trans-Continental Fiber Tunnel (TCFT). The TCFT
Project, funded in part by your federal tax dollars,
promises to dramatically enhance the sustained
livability of Americans like you throughout the entire
US West Extended Customer Service Area. Now that
FCC approval of the implementation phase of this
joint project has been granted, technicians from US
West will soon be visiting your home to install the
portion of the TCFT that passes through your
children. Please read over the included Q&A text at
the end of this letter to find out more. This is an
exciting opportunity for all of us, and we at US West
want to keep you well-informed.

Sincerely,
All Of Us At US West.

● ● ●

QUESTIONS AND ANSWERS ABOUT THE
TRANS-CONTINENTAL FIBER TUNNEL
(TCFT):

Q: Through which of my children will the TCFT
pass?
A: Yolanda, Matthew and Aimee. Jack will not be
affected by this installation procedure.

Q: What steps are being taken to assure the safety and
health of my family during this procedure?
A: US West's trained staff of network engineers, ditch
implementors and customer support representatives
will be available 24-hours during and after the
installation, via our toll-free customer support hotline:
1-800-WE-CARE-0 (zero).

Q: What will the installation look like?
A: Upon completion, the TCFT will resemble a
four-inch (10.3-centimeter) diameter aluminum pipe,
fixtured to the north-east side breakfast nook wall,
passing in a straight horizontal line through your
kitchenette area, dining room, and TV room, before
exiting your home just to the left of your sofa. The
pipe will traverse at an altitude of 38 inches (97
centimeters) from your floor. The pipe will also pass
through the upper shoulder area of Aimee (13), the
face and rear-cranial area of Yolanda (9) and will graze
the ear of Matthew (7.5).

Q: Why is it crucial that the TCFT intersect my home and family in this fashion?
A: Strict design and budgetary constraints dictated by our federally mandated business plan prohibit the complexity of design that would be required to re-implement the TCFT conduit around your domicile. Instead a shortest-path algorithm has been approved by the Federal Communications Oversight Authority and members of your community. If you would like to discuss these impacts of excessive telecommunications regulation with your senator or representative, call our toll-free congressional hotline: 1-800-SMRT-VTR.

Q: Will my regular telephone service be interrupted during the installation procedure?
A: No.

Q: Will the health of my family be negatively impacted by the TCFT installation?
A: This is not directly foreseen. US West recognizes that the health of your loved ones is an important family concern. We offer a toll-free informational service you may use to learn more about family nutrition, troubleshooting basic illness, and how to shop for the best deal in health insurance. Simply dial: 1-800-DOC-TALK.

Q: What is US West doing to compensate families for the inconvenience brought about by the TCFT?

A: US West is always striving to better serve the community. The TCFT project benefits all of us, through increased access to on-demand digital television programming, new interactive shopping opportunities, and an expanded intra-community citizen data system shared by firemen, health officials, and community safety officials. This network, known as NARCNET, promises to dramatically upspeed the processing of 911 emergency calls, and may save lives. US West understands that the TCFT installation process will be inconvenient for you, and we have chosen to offer a free gift to you and other affected customers in the service area. To claim your free gift, dial our toll-free giftline: 1-800-PAY-OFFS.

Magic Pill

This is the one time in my life that I feel able to lift
ten times my own weight in sagging plastic bags of old
clothing. This is the one time in my life that birds
swooping down from nearby trees to pick at my hair
do not bother me so much. This is the dawn of a
bright, fantastic new day. This is the first time that I've
ever had the courage to drive my car without first
attaching the lap and shoulder belts. I have never felt
electricity actually buzzing up and down my back and
along my shoulders and the backs of my arms and
down my legs and into my hands and feet and fingers
and toes before. Today time is composed of moments,
and each moment is palpable and exists as a heartbeat,
a tick in a perfect clock, orderly, one after the other,
and my movements and my thoughts are listening to
the beat of movements, and synchronized, and dancing
with it, and everything that happens is graceful, orderly
and correct. It's like I am a bell that has been struck,
and is ringing a pure tone. I can fly. I can breathe
underwater. I can leave my body. I can have sex with
supermodels. I can live forever. I can radiate energy,
laserlike, from my eyes. I can win at video poker. I
can fix my own car. I can withstand extremes of heat
and cold. I can climb up trees. I can do anything. 👁

The Fun We Tried To Have

We got some beers and put them in the trunk. We
scored some drugs. We filled the tires and the tank
and the windshield washer fluid reservoir and we
picked everybody up and headed for the ocean. It was
a beautiful day when we left. Rebecca was on the rag
and made a big deal of explaining to all of us
beforehand about how awful it was going to be to be
around her, not really apologizing or anything, just
warning us in advance that she was unlikely to have or
be or create much fun. She had this scruntchy tension
in her face, knotted up and squinting through her
thick glasses. Kevin was quiet. He brought his guitar
but there wasn't enough space in the back seat for his
guitar with everybody else coming, so he put it in the
trunk. James was there, and Scott and Sparrow, who
together managed to overturn any suggestion of what
music to play on the tape deck, so instead we listened
to the radio. Keith hates commercials, so he kept
flipping channels, reaching over Angie's knees to hit
the scan button, so all we heard was halves of songs,
halves of conversations, and little fragments of really
annoying commercials. I drove.

Rebecca explained how because she was on the rag she
would need to stop frequently to use unsanitary service
station bathrooms in order to change her tampons,
enough of which she was pretty sure she hadn't
brought, and that using said restrooms was the sort of
experience that you would find depressing and
humiliating even if you weren't on the rag, nevertheless,
it was very urgent that we pull over at a service station,
and not just any unclean-looking one but either an
Arco or a Chevron or a BP. So we found a BP and she

hopped out, and everybody hopped out and Keith went inside to buy a candy bar, and pretty soon everybody was inside having a candy bar except for me and Scott who grabbed beers from the case in the trunk and went in search of a private place to pound them.

It turned out that this BP had only outdoor plastic chemical porta-toilets, but Rebecca informed us that she didn't want to create problems or seem ungrateful or bring everybody down, so she would just hold it until we got to the beach. We all got back into the car, and everybody had a soda and Keith spilled his soda on Angie's lap, and so they got out again and Keith got Angie some paper towels that sopped up some of it, but Angie was cool about it, incredibly cool considering I knew she didn't really want to go on this trip at all, but came along to be with me, and being there was determined to enjoy herself, which is one of those things about her that I love her for. So she laughed it off, and everybody started joking around a little bit, except for Rebecca, and we all got back on the road and got underway.

Then we hit some traffic, some sort of road construction, and slowed to an occasional creep. It got hot. We rolled up the windows and turned on the A/C but the A/C had a bad smell of mildew and people got nauseous so we turned it off and rolled the windows back down. Traffic continued to almost not move for another half-hour. We drank all of the water — there was only a gallon for all seven of us, and all of our sodas were also gone, and all of the ice in them, and the paper cups and plastic lids and straws were crunching up on the freshly cleaned carped below. We were thirsty and hot. We all knew there was a case of beer in the trunk, cooling in a cooler full of ice, and I knew it was going to come to that, but as the driver and the one whose license was at stake I didn't like the idea too much. Also the car behind us had a cell-phone, and there were "Report Drunken Drivers 1-800-SAV-A-LIF" signs every twenty miles or so. As we crept closer and began to round a corner, I saw three lanes of traffic trying to merge together into one lane in a very tight space, and beyond that I saw a long row of cop cars and two ambulances, and just beyond that I started to see some wreckage.

Keith pointed out that if we were going to get the beers out of the trunk we ought to do it soon before we were any closer to all those cops. And he yanked the keys out of the ignition and jumped out and went around and pulled the big blue box that reads Pabst Blue Ribbon Par-T-Pak legibly from 100 feet away out of the trunk and slammed the trunk lid harder than it needs to be slammed and hopped back in the car and slammed that door, also unnecessarily hard, and gave everybody a beer, and I had one too. They were cold and good. Then he tried to hide the rest of the case of beer under his feet with limited success.

We continued to creep slowly forward. We had been there nearly an hour. Rebecca said nothing and the look on her face told me I would need to stop at the next available service station featuring sanitary indoor toilet facilities, and it better be soon. She had no beer. The three-lane merge was horrible. Everybody honked

at everybody, people just leaned on their horns
non-stop, as two gigantic Winnebagos together
blocked off the mergers from the left so that a long
row of other Winnebagos could cut in front of the rest
of traffic. The cops didn't seem to notice or care.
They were everywhere, chattering into the radios on
their shoulders, looking very serious and kind of
agitated. Eventually we got around the corner some
more and the one wrecked car I had seen became two,
three, five wrecked cars, and a motorcycle, and further
on there was a rescue team surrounding another
smaller car.

We crept on, heads craned out the window. I just
wanted to go away, but even after we got merged
together into one lane the traffic continued to crawl.
Keith saw something, and then Kevin and Sparrow saw
it, and then I saw it: underneath a red hatchback that
had rolled on its driver's side, an arm stuck out at an
angle that couldn't have left it attached to anything.
And tucked behind the hatchback, kind of hidden, an
opaque brown plastic bag covered something dead and
person-shaped on the ground, and there was a large
fluorescent orange sticker affixed to it that said
REMAINS. We all got very quiet and drank more
beer and tried to stop looking. We crawled on past
four more smashed cars. You could see by the scrapes
and scratches on the road that they had all been
dragged aside by trucks. One old Volvo had a
head-impact shatter on the windshield, bloody brown,
and the entire front end was smashed into a wedge like
it had tried to fit under some other car. And the Volvo
had a bag on the ground behind it too.

Rebecca screamed Let me out! Open the Door and we tried to calm her down but she bolted over Sparrow and out the door and began to run around in a circle, looking for something that wasn't there that she desperately needed, and then as she twisted she threw up all over the roadside next to us in a long ugly arc of vomit. And then Scott got out of the car nonchalantly on the right rear side, and I watched him in the right-side mirror as he threw up neatly in the roadside on top of part of where Rebecca threw up, and then the car behind us stopped and a fat lady opened her door and didn't even get out, just puked right there next to her car and shut the door again. I got very queasy myself. Then suddenly the cars in front of us got some speed and started taking off, and the lady in the car behind us leaned on her horn, and some of the police started looking towards us, so we all got back in the car and drove on.

We finally got back to three lanes and traffic was thinner than ever, and we all felt kind of awful. I stopped at the next BP, but Rebecca said she didn't need anything and just wanted to go, and everybody got pissed off at me for stopping without any need to stop. So we got back on the road. We were about thirty miles from the beach, and the sky was getting cloudy. The car reeked of beer and the cans were littered all over the floor. I asked everybody to pick up the trash and put it in the beer box, and a couple of people halfheartedly picked up a few things.

Kevin then said Does anybody want some pot? And Sparrow said Oh got I NEED some pot! and everybody concurred. I didn't say anything. I felt a little bit light-headed but I was just not wanting to worry anybody, or bum anybody out, or bring anybody down, or further threaten the enjoyability of our Sunday at the beach, which we had planned for a week and which was perhaps our last chance where all seven of us would be free on the same Sunday, our last fun-trip of that summer. I just wanted everybody to stop feeling bad and start having a good time. Kevin loaded his big glass pipe and passed it around the car. I wasn't going to smoke any myself, but then I did.

And then it was like we all finally started to relax and enjoy each other's company. Finally. Keith invented a new game, called "Pileup", in which the back-seat inhabitants would attempt to form a pile of mangled human bodies as in a car wreck. They would have ten seconds to arrange themselves, and then they had to Freeze while Keith took polaroids for insurance purposes. Everybody had the best dead-mangled faces. Then Kevin started singing Two Dozen Beers Six Sodas And Four Buds On The Wall, Two Dozen Beers Six Sodas And Four Buds ... and we sang that for a while, and then we broke into several simultaneous conversations about various fascinating topics. I just got into driving, and meditated on each driving maneuver, and kept my speed at exactly the legal limit and practiced staying perfectly and unwaveringly in-lane. The sky became dark grey but nobody really noticed. You could begin to smell the sea. We'd be there soon.

And when we got there, the fun we would have. Real American summertime Fun, the kind we used to have all the time, the kind we are always complaining that we never have any more. It makes life bearable, this Fun, the elaborate and time-consuming and crowded and dangerous and intoxicated pursuit of it. I began to realize that for all my efforts at calmness and concentration, I couldn't tell if I was staying inside my lane or not. My eyes were jerked around by details on the roadside as we drove. Signs for smoked fish outlets, and garage sales, and explanations of local parking policy. We passed a dying shed with a dying Japanese pickup truck next to it. And then up ahead, on the right side, next to a large gravelly turn-out I saw a hippie with his thumb out, and I always pick up hippies. So I automatically flipped the turn signal and started pulling to the side of the road, and slowing down, or so I thought. Keith said Woah there when I got the right side onto the gravel. Rebecca made a squeak noise. The hippie was looking right at me. He was skinny and had a little mustache and long black hair with beads or something in it. He was stepping back from the roadside. I realized I was still moving kind of fast.

So I applied a bit more brake, and then I had the strangest sensation of the entire globe beneath us being spun in circles while we remained in the car, completely still. I had my seat belt on. Someone started screaming about three seconds into the spin, I think it was Angie. Everybody else was transfixed. I gripped the wheel and sort of spun it left and right in a futile effort as the road that used to be behind us came around from our left, crossed our right, and then the bank of trees, and then right dead ahead of us, the hippie again, who leapt up off the ground quite amazingly, rose above us and landed in some condition on the roof. Then our spin ended with a metallic shock to the rear right side, and we were again attached to the earth. Angie stopped screaming.

We all checked, we all seemed to be okay. I got out and looked at the hippie, who was sitting on his ass on the slightly dented roof, just staring at me with fear in his eyes. I asked, are you hurt? He didn't say anything, but he slowly slid down the back window onto the trunk lid, which had popped loose and flapped under him, and then to the ground, where he stood. Everybody was getting our of the car at this point, looking around them. Behind us, coming from the roadway, the skid we'd made was angular and crazy, didn't even look like a car's tracks. Keith said, What the fuck was that all about? I wandered around to the right-hand side of the car, where it had struck some concrete-filled steel post that jutted up to protect some kind of gas or water metering equipment that rose out of the earth, sprouted a set of dials and boxes, and then sank back underground.

Then I decided I would like to lie down, so I laid down on the gravel and stared up into the overcast sky. We had to be mere inches from the sea by now, the smell was everywhere. Everybody crowded around me quite suddenly, shouting Mike, Mike, what's wrong, Mike? Wake up! No fun, I said. Mike, did you faint? This is no fun. We had all the tools of Fun, and we had a Fun Plan and the will to achieve it, and a Funmobile, and yet there is no fun. Where did it go? I thought I caught a drop of water in my right eye.

That dude's drunk! I heard a voice say, it was the hippie, the guy I wanted to provide a lift to. I got up off the ground and felt suddenly totally sober. Hey man, I said, I'm really extremely sorry. I was pulling over to give you a lift and I think I had a blowout. Are you all right?

He looked at me very intensely, at my clothing, at my face, at my car. I said: I'm fine now, I just fainted for a minute. From the shock, I think. Are you okay?

He was pretty obviously okay, just standing there looking at me. I said: do you still need a ride?

Thanks, dude, but I don't really wanna ride with you, he said.

I said, Okay, do you need a doctor or anything?

I'm not sure brah, I'm just ... kind of broke, that's all.

We ended up giving him sixty bucks for no particular reason except because I had almost killed him, and I gave him my name and address and phone number so he could come back and sue me later. Keith and I decided that the trip might go smoother if he drove the rest of the way. So he managed to rip the car free of the post — the body panels had sort of crumpled in around both sides of it, so it took some extensive forward-and-reverse to free the vehicle — and we decided that while the cosmetic damage was pretty gory, the frame was still straight and the tires were intact and no crucial systems were damaged except the right rear taillight, and of course the trunk latch. We didn't have any rope to tie it closed with, but Kevin said we could use his guitar strap, so Scott went to get it out of the trunk. Kevin said No, I'll get it, then Scott said No, really, he'd get it, and Kevin said Wait a minute, my guitar, and Scott, who had already had a look in there, didn't say anything. Kevin had a look in the trunk, came back with the guitar strap and part of the guitar neck still tied to it, and that about killed off all the remaining fun.

We all felt sick. Rebecca hadn't said a word during the entire spinout debacle. She stood by herself near the edge of the clearing, facing into the clearing and away from us. At one point the hippie tried to make some small talk with her. I saw him approach and then stop and turn around and march resignedly back to the roadside, apparently due to something she'd muttered under her breath. Moments later, a VW Jetta with a cell-phone antenna pulled over and picked the hippie up. A woman in the back seat, cradling the phone to her ear, eyed us maliciously. It occurred to me that we had been there a while and ought to get going. It was late afternoon. Kevin tied up the trunk hatch with the entrails of his guitar. I climbed into the back seat middle position, the "Lucky Pierre" position which nobody usually wants, and we all got back in the car except for Rebecca. Keith honked the horn and called her name, but she ignored him. He got out and talked to her for about ten minutes, during which time at least one police car slowed down while passing us on the highway. He came back and explained that Rebecca had decided to stay. There was a brief discussion, but Keith started the car and backed up near the roadside, then put the gears in Drive in order to depart. We watched Rebecca, but she was still turned away. I thought I saw a weird brownish blotch on her butt, but it occurred to me that it was probably just dust from sitting in the roadside dirt.

Keith began to pull into traffic, and then James and Sparrow protested that we couldn't just leave her, we had to take her with us, by force if necessary. So Keith pulled off the road again, honked at loudly by a semi as he did so. James and Sparrow got out of both back doors, walked over to where Rebecca was sitting at the edge of the clearing, head in her hands, and then Scott got out, and walked over there, and I watched as together, on some signal, they all actually grabbed her and started to haul her struggling body back to the car. She screamed earnestly. Scott got her torso from behind and James and Sparrow each held one kicking leg. She screamed some more, and another cop car, or perhaps it was the same cop car, drove past us again very slowly.

Rebecca's kicking and screaming body was hurled on top of me, and James and Sparrow climbed in on either side of us, preventing escape. Then Rebecca bit my hand. And it fucking hurt.

Doors slammed, engine gunned, Keith pulled rapidly into traffic as the back-seat struggle continued. James was on the right, taking Rebecca's shoes off and trying to tickle her feet. She thrashed violently, kicked Scott in the back of the head and gashed James' cheek with a red-painted toenail. She chewed savagely on my hand, right between the thumb and forefinger, muttering invective as she did so, and Scott for some reason decided it would be smart to start spanking her stained and odd-smelling butt with the plastic map-holding envelope from the glove box, which split open, being antique, and spilled maps all over us, and then Rebecca got some of Keith's hair and started pulling it, and Keith screamed and swerved and the tires squealed a bit, and that's when everybody froze for a second ... and then Rebecca stopped struggling and started weeping and wailing and screaming, and continued to do so for a while.

Pretty soon we got to Seaside, the little town next to the beach we like to have fun at. Keith asked if we should get anything, and Rebecca said she really, really, really, really needed a bathroom, and please, please, please, please, could she have one. And so we stopped at the little M&P gas market there by the main town road, and Rebecca climbed out, assumed some composure, and went inside. Then Scott got out and went inside as well, and pretty soon everybody was inside, milling around in a weird mood, saying nothing at all, picking up idle bits of snack food and squeezing them. Scott bought another case of beer. The shopkeeper was an old Korean woman, who seemed pretty nervous to have us all in the store at the same time, milling about, not talking, not looking at her, picking things up off the shelves and then putting them back in the wrong places. Eventually everybody bought a candy bar. We waited outside in the car for Rebecca, and she took a long time but eventually emerged, slowly, with dignity intact, and got back in the car without argument, still saying nothing. Wet splotches at this point were appearing regularly on the windshield.

When we got to the beach proper it was about five p.m., windy and cold and continuing to begin to rain. We had planned on some sunbathing, but instead decided we would build a fire. Kevin said that he wanted to burn his guitar, but James said that his guitar could be fixed, and then Kevin showed James some parts of the guitar, and James had no reply. So we all wandered around the beach collecting bits of wood, all of which were moist and wouldn't light too well.

Rebecca said: Wow, now we are finally having Fun, the sarcasm was thick in her voice, My good friends and I are at the beach having Fun! Then Scott started yelling at Rebecca about how she had (apparently) insisted upon coming along, but once along had done everything in her power to bring everybody down and be a nuisance, and she said So I made Mike drink and smoke dope and try to run down a hitchhiker? And on and on. Nobody had the energy, really, to argue with Rebecca about her attitude. We were all in a coma, finally arrived, not wanting to do anything except stay warm. We all wanted to be home, but none of us wanted to get back in the car. So we gathered wood.

Scott and Keith and James together piled the wood in a weird-shaped stack, and tore up the empty beer case box for kindling, leaving the beer cans all over the floor of the car. The case itself was also fairly soaked with spilled beer. Kevin added the broken remains of his guitar, sticking them in the pyre at odd angles, which disintegrated the structure of the heap — it all collapsed. It didn't seem to me like any of them knew how to build a fire, and they assumed masks of fake confidence while building it which assured me it wasn't ever going to get lit. When I was a child, as a Boy Scout, I earned a Webelo patch for starting perfect campfires out of damp wood. But after almost killing everybody, I didn't feel safe near open flame.

They fiddled with it, using their lighters that went out instantly in the windy rain, Scott, Keith, Kevin, James, the men-folk, while the women-folk, Sparrow, Angie, Rebecca, stood to one side telling them they were doing it wrong. I went to clean the beer cans out of the car, and got more and more pissed off as I started really thinking about how badly I had fucked up, how much work it would take to fix the car, and about how my so-called friends litter trash all over said car like it's their personal dumpster. I pulled cans out of every crack and space, and stomped them into little disks on the ground beneath the driver's side door.

Angie came over and stood by me, saying nothing as I picked cups and lids and straws and wrappers out of the Funmobile. She took my hand. We got in the back seat together and laid down, her on top of me, and we just laid there staying warm and not talking, for a while. We kissed, and she nuzzled my ear with her nose.

Scott came back to the car and stuck his head in, and said that they had all been talking and that the general consensus was that this was the most horrible fucked-up day in recent memory and that everybody wanted to go home and sulk, and what did I think? I agreed that going home and sulking sounded like a fun idea. So we all got back in the car and drove home, silently, not stopping once, as heavy rain continued to fall, and the wind whistled through the twisted body holes, and we played no music on the stereo and told no jokes and did no drugs and picked up no hitchhikers and when we got back to my place they all went their separate ways, and Angie and I went to sleep, and the next day we went to work early in the morning and that was no fun either. 👁

Story Problem:

i was like, this letter, number, okay, i just invented my
own math. that's what i do a lot, actually. what i
hate is when i get like a bad test and everything's like
adding, subtracting, multiplying six. 860/6 instead of
putting like one, i latched a zero, so i put thirty
instead of like three so i got points knocked off like
that. that was really complicated math like that i
finally got down i hate that! yeah. well it's hard to
tell if he doesn't let you use ... Mr. Molnard won't let
us use a calculator on that test, for those equations ...
i can't check if it's like that. those two problems are
going to be worth 30 points. it's friday. it's friday? i
can't sleep! you should go in 7th grade to make up ...
i seriously have no idea ...

so that's like ... i don't take French anymore. oh that's
right. sorry. who else is going? did you already turn
in your thing? it's due today? oh well, i'll be like ...
that's what i thought ... my dad's like why do you have
to go and ... health, personal stuff ... why are you
asking me these questions? i don't know. underneath
you write three. so we have to find like ...

this is a right triangle, right there, so let that g h g
cosine equals ... do you know what i mean? okay, forty
times three is nine forty point two eight, feet per
second okay. we'll ask him this morning. forty
degrees. cosine forty times 940 point two eight yeah i
will. i can tell these are your drawings. it's not bad, it's
just ... the little flowers ... those aren't mine, i didn't
draw them. and then if he asks, like if you did that,
say, i don't know, you tell me! that one thing he

114

showed us you know the angles, the right angles, good job guys.

i'm going to have friends because of math. seriously monster nightmare story problems, you know what, i hate story problems the most out of all math. i can do the logic with Mr. Gatter. i love logic. i love that kind of stuff, but it's like either that or that, figuring it out. is this logical? no, it's not. looking at a problem and being able to say what, is where, how to do it, and i like, i know how to do like, rectangles, totally know how to do that, airplane and wind problems, i think i know how to do, but when i read this problem i don't go okay, equal measures, the cosine, blah blah okay that's easy. forty second? my brother ... what's um one down? it's two O's sorry, over and over, present has two Rs, another holiday they have two Rs though ha ha okay, two down it's enough. water. s o s? what? everything is land, how? i do that, i do that, 80 degrees where'd my picture go? see, i always do problems harder than i need, i have no idea. soft moonlight ... blue moon in the sky ... this is like the back, for, let's, spoken, huh? yeah. it seems to me like, did you? Mr. Wright yesterday said like, it was the last day, i had it all filled out, i wrote his, more involved? i'm sorry. i'm so sad cause ... i love Mr. Wright. let's just ask him for problems four through five, you know, just convert this so it's our times six plus two equals nine, no we have to add, i can't add, so it's nineteen, twenty, all right, see, i just always oh, but i just do, nineteen? the tangent? here, square root, no that's, yeah, we added four and twelve. no, this is for

converting oh it's nega— it's inverse here, negative one,
so it's ten to the negative one of what? like, sixteen M?
point four, four point one four, fifteen over nineteen?
there are bad things ... the blues ... what's the other
one? twenty point four eighteen, square root, right.
what's the no name for ... the blues will come and
they'll find you ... dinner problem? yeah! the blues ...
if you're born with, you'll die with, the blues, think
what you choose ... the happy beat in your if you can't
pay the dues ... with the blues ... do ba bum bee doo,
dey boo ... aaaaa! i hate story problems! 👁

ADVERTISEMENT

ARE YOU STONED? MSL invites you to take this
simple test. One: are you already finding this
incredibly funny? Like, are you laughing out loud
right now? Two: are you unable to figure out why it is
that you're still reading this, and yet you feel oddly
compelled to keep reading, and furthermore to OBEY?
Three: are you finding you finding yourself easily
yourself confused? Five: are you having trouble
keeping your place in this paragraph? Five: are all of
the people in the room with you noticing the fact that
you are saying your answers to these questions out loud
and giggling and snorting, and are they glaring at you?
Eight: are these people watching you? Are they
thinking that you are a loser for being such a huge
stoner? Seven: have you noticed how they all seem to
be able to talk to each other telepathically? Can you
hear what they're saying? Eight: do your toesie-woesies
feel tingle-wingle? Nine: have you just masturbated, or
are you thinking about masturbating, or ... eeew, are
you masturbating right now? My god, you are such a
freak. Sure. Go ahead, masturbate. I give you
permission. Just keep reading these questions. Ten:
Okay, are you masturbating? Good. Eleven: do you
believe in God? Twelve: is the feeling that you get
when you masturbate similar to the feeling you get
from God? Thirteen: is your buzz wearing off? Maybe
you should smoke some more pot. Fourteen: are you
watching television? What are you watching? Isn't
TV fascinating? Fifteen: is there something that you're
supposed to be doing right now that you've been
putting off for a while, that you thought you might do
today, except that you got stoned instead and now it's

out of the question? Sixteen: do you believe that smoking pot affects your concentration? Seventeen: hello? Eighteen: are you susceptible to intense feelings of worthlessness and low self-esteem? Eighteen: do you think there might be a connection there, someplace, between all that pot that you smoke and your inability to do anything with your life and your bad, unhappy negative feelings? Nineteen: is it all too much to think about? Twenty: are you loading another bowl? Twenty-One: isn't it funny how you can know what the problem is but not be able to do anything about the problem? Twenty-Two: don't you wish someone would just tell you what to do to escape from this trap? Twenty-Three: would you believe the MSL Catalog is the solution? Twenty-Four: no, seriously, I know a guy who's a brain surgeon, he's constantly stoned but he reads the MSL Catalog and he's got a loving wife and three kids, and he wins awards and shit. Twenty-Five: wouldn't you like to be like that guy? Or like this other guy I know who ordered a bunch of stuff out of the MSL Catalog, and now he's a famous artist in LA and makes lots of money and has groupies. Twenty-Six: how much would you pay for this miraculous Catalog, which is available mail-order for a fee? Twenty-Seven: how much is salvation worth to you? Twenty-Eight: send a dollar and a self-addressed stamped envelope to:

PLEASE RESCUE ME FROM MY LIFESTYLE
MSL
5536 NE 27TH AVE
PORTLAND, OR 97211-6230 👁

Need More Energy!

Now I'm doing jumping jacks! Because my writing needs more energy! ENERGY! It must SEAR! It must TINGLE! Raw emotion — screams of the unconscious — the screwdriver of desire jammed in the toaster of human misery! Aaaah! Now I am hitting myself on the head! On the HEAD! With a hammer! A HAMMER! I am striking blows of freedom against my own complacency! Oooch! Aaah! It hurts!

Not enough ... not ... ENOUGH! NEED MORE ENERGY! Heart must explode — brain must shut down — pure reflex takes over — the reptilian mind tells no lies! Now I'm in the Congo, our safari is lost, the insects swarm and pester ... the million mindless creatures of the carpet and the carapace are singing their insanity ... Madness haunts us! Reflex only! Abandon rationality! From behind the bluff, the lion springs! Instant! Danger! What are the words! To type! To fend off! This monstrous creature! Combat words! Bladed sentences! Pointy consonants! Like the letter X! Letter X now! Another! XXX! Letter X forever or we are DOOMED!

No! Too late! Not soon enough! How to escape this shell of convention? How to break through to the surface? Honesty is our submarine — dignity is our iceberg — ENERGY is our Polaris missile! Melt the ice caps! MELT THEM NOW! MELT THEM!

More ENERGY! More POWER! More FEELING! I am sticking my penis in the light socket now! Soon I will flip the switch! Then ... then I will suffer for my DREAM! Then I will taste what it means to be ALIVE! I am flipping the switch! NOW! OOOOOOOOOH! PAINFUL! Is this what pain means? To be in pain, always hurting, hurting always, hurting from the agonizing PAIN? STOP THE PAIN! STOP THE MADNESS! OW! OW! OW! OW! OW!

I am driving now. I am driving faster. I am driving faster still. I am approaching the speed of light. 55 ... 60 ... 61 ... faster and faster! The speed, it does something for me — it makes me feel FAST. 65 ... 70 ... 75 ... the fuselage is shaking! The rear view mirror vibrates menacingly, as if it could at any moment DETACH and SHRIEK through the air, or splinter into a thousand fragments, or splinter and THEN SHRIEK! 80 ... 85 ... I didn't know a Fiesta could go this fast ... I am EXCITED! I am ENERGETIC! My life is ACTION-PACKED, and so is my writing! I feel ALIVE! I feel MACHO! I have neglected to slow down for this turn! I have no insurance, but I must SKID!

energy energy energy energy ENERGY more more more more MORE! Now I'm snorting crystal methedrine — up my NOSE! My NOSE! More pain ... yes! pain is good ... more pain ... ow! ... okay, that's enough pain. Now I'm drinking lots of COFFEE, to take the edge off the speed. Now I'm eating lots of SANDWICHES to take the edge off the coffee. I'm feeling the effect, the effect is happening to me now. My mind is accelerating ... but I'm not getting any smarter! I'm thinking the same thoughts over and over like before, only FASTER! Now I'm taking a DRAG off a REEFER CIGARETTE! Wow man, far out! More sandwiches! Now I'm DROPPING ACID! I'm taking a postage stamp that someone sold me for twenty bucks and I'm licking all the paste off of it and sticking it on my forehead! I'm waiting for the effect ... I anticipate WONDERFUL NEW THINGS ... I wonder what plaid will smell like? But I have no patience — I am a man of ACTION! While I wait for the acid to kick in I run outside and start asking people where I can get some heroin! I ask them all! I must know! The police come and I am ARRESTED! Soon I will write my lengthy prison opus! I am so EXCITED!

Now I'm learning what it means to kill! To pluck the mortality from an earthly carriage! To hear the HSSSSSSSS sound as the soul escapes the body. I have killed all of the bugs in my house, and I'm trying to decide what to kill next. I want to kill something more dangerous, like a plague-bearing rat, or maybe a black widow spider. And I want to kill larger things, like antelopes and houses and continents. I want to find the most dangerous planet in the solar system and KILL IT in the name of ADVENTURE! What planet should I kill? Which one is most savage? Now I'm hard at work in my laboratory ... I am designing the PLANETARY PERSONALITY PROFILE. Were you lonely and unloved during gaseous collapse? Is your surface covered with a thick layer of boiling phosphoric acid and toxic fumes, anathema to all life as we know it? If a moon left your orbit, what steps would you take to bring it back? No ... this takes too long. I am a man of ACTION! I live an active LIFESTYLE! I will kill VENUS, because it's closest. Now I am at the survival store. Maybe I should kill someone here. But no, that won't work, we're all SURVIVORS here. We can only kill things that don't shop here. I am at the survival store, shopping, surviving. I am shopping for a telescope and the largest crossbow I can buy. Bah! This crossbow is PUNY! I will buy an assault rifle instead. Now all I need is a HUGE LADDER ...

I must be more REAL. I must exist HARDER! My writing must be a testament to TRUTH, to a life that WAS and still IS. When I die I want people to be able to read what I wrote and say: until he died he was ALIVE. And now that he's dead, he's just not the same. Everyone dies, but some of us put it off until the last minute. I must have a good life, and after that a good death. I have to die ... ENERGETICALLY! I must leap into the clutches of death like a trapeze artist leaps bravely into the outstretched arms of his partner, unflinching, unafraid even knowing that if I miscalculate even slightly I might fall to the ground and be KILLED! I want to die like Hemmingway was planning to die before he accidentally tripped on his bearskin rug while yawning and tumbled forward onto that shotgun he was in the process of cleaning. Such tragedy won't be my fate! I want to look death in the eyes, and say: here death, here deathie deathie death, come to Papa. I want death to come when I call, and

sit in my lap and eat out of my hand ... no! Too
effeminate! I want death to come when I call, obey my
commands, fear my wrath ... and then gnash me to
pieces in its mighty jaws! Slowly! PAINFULLY! And
with PANACHE!

But not yet! Not today! Because I'm a young writer
with ENERGY, and I've got a lot of young energetic
writing left in me. I've got BURNING REAMS of
BRILLIANT FIRE to put out! Lyric blood to spurt
from my HEART! Babies of genius to birth!
Gallstones of insight yet to pass! Organs of theory still
to DONATE! Limbs of autobiography yet to ensnare
in the offset press of destiny! If I seem to boast, it's
because my view of the truth is unclouded by petty
facts and knowledge. I may appear scatterbrained, but
in truth I'm OMNITHOUGHTFUL! I seem
lethargic, but really I'm just COILED! And when I
finally burst onto the front pages of the literary
supplement of history, my bio will be big and fat and
fast and pulsing with life. It will read: He is so bright
and strong and powerful a writer, you could run ten
blenders off the manic twitching of his brow as he
writes! You could fry eggs on the red-hot surface of his
typewriter! You could use his stiff cock to roll pasta!
But you wouldn't because he never sits still — he's just
got too much god damn ENERGY!!! 👁

The Restaurant With Dead
People Hanging From The Ceiling

We went to that restaurant you told us about, the one
where all the dead people are hanging from the ceiling,
their heads lodged in the plaster so that they seem like
the underside of a people-garden, or like accreted fleshy
stalactites. Yes, pretty weird ... but the food is
incredible! You were right, they really know veal. It's
funny, when we got there we sort of wondered
whether, I mean, we wanted to know how they got
that effect, you know ... it's just really well-done. They
look real. They look like real live dead people lodged
in the actual ceiling. But of course you'd smell them if
they were real ... Did you notice that some of them
twitch from time to time? It's like they must have
robotic parts or something.

But yeah, we had the Veal Scallopini and it was just
perfect, plus we had the white bean and spinach
bruschettas, excellent, with a little bit of cumin. And
our waiter was so funny! You know they're all actors.
He did this thing, where he acted very friendly but
kind of nervous ... it was like he was pretending,
basically, that there were real dead people hanging from
the ceiling, and that he himself was a prisoner in the
place and extremely scared but trying to hide his
nervousness behind a professional demeanor. It was a
riot! We played along, of course, and told him we
would send for help when we left, after he slipped us
this hilarious note, "Help Help Get Me Out Of Here
You Are My Only Hope," et cetera, and we left him a
big tip. I hope the place catches on because the
concept is just brilliant.

126

And the desserts! Excellent! And we had this bottle of wine from Spain, not one I'd heard of but it packed a wallop, for sure. That kind of intense almost fizzy bite at the bottom of it, but very very subtle. The tiniest taste of the strongest flavor, you know. Those tables there are made from real bones, too! Did you know that? Dave was with us, who's in med school, he seemed entranced by the furniture in particular. We thought they were probably all cow and pig bones, but he assured us they were mostly human bones. Dave says that human skeletons are pretty easy to get, and they did look like they had all been sanitized pretty well. Bleached, one assumes.

It's true the whole place is kind of macabre. But at the same time they've got real flair. They've got lovely dried flowers arranged everywhere, and the tables are always set with starched white cloth, and even though we were the only ones there that evening (I do hope more people find out about the place!) it had this spirited, public feeling. Like the headless bodies hanging from the ceiling are a metaphor for the experiences of society. You know, they're the anonymous mass, the people you don't know or notice but who are just there.

I'm excited, really, to see more restaurants taking risks like this. The avant-garde dining scene in this city is so moribund! If you read this note any time soon, let's go there again and bring Andy and Claire, okay? And where have you been, anyway? I've been trying to reach you by phone for days. Call me, okay? 👁

The Wreck of the Indescribable Thing

I open my eyes and all I see is the deepest blue, too
pure and deep to be the sky, too wide and complete to
be anything but the sky. Wind blows past my ears, but
the silence is that much more complete because of it.
A blob, an orb covered with rags and windows and
water and skin and dirty hairs and dust and drugs
wanders into my field of view far above, it's like a giant
hot air balloon, slowly cruising over me some fifteen
thousand feet away, hovering there. I wonder if it
will land.

"Oh shit!" it says, and I remember again how to say
Oh Shit is to say nothing at all, except that you've
realized something you can't express yet. But I am at
peace here, hypnotized by peace. I have no past or
future, I do not exist. I wonder for a moment what
my name might be, but trying to use that part of my
head is painful, like trying to scratch with a broken
finger. I back off, and return to peace.

Ah. Peace.

Footsteps. Somewhere to my left or right. I have
some awareness that I am probably lying on the
ground and not floating, as my body feels it's floating,
magically three feet above it, though I am confident
that if I need to levitate at any moment, I'll just
levitate, no problem, there won't be any hassle or
performance anxiety or uncertainty. It will be fine.
Everything will be fine, and the only reason I'm not
levitating right now is that I don't feel like it, because
nothing could be nicer, nothing could improve upon

how and where I am, right now.

But somehow I know that this peace can't last, as I hear more footsteps now, and see another hot air balloon, this one close-cropped and red and covered with wrap-around sunglasses and face-paint. What does this second airship have to add? "Oh fucking shit!" You are always amazed at the ineloquence of people at moments of bliss. But let them be. They are good and happy, and even as more footsteps approach and I realize a crowd of balloons is forming, and that they are come to wake me from my beautiful dream, I decide, okay, now that I understand the meaning of everything and how to levitate and live forever and achieve total peace, I know I can come back here at any time, so I let go, pay my respects to the blue sky and turn my head to the right.

There is a ring of people looking down at me, and they are all the funniest looking people you could imagine, half of them are naked and not just naked but erotically disenclothed by hunks of steel stuck through them, by tight butt-cheek-shaping straps, by paintings on their bodies. They are all looking at me. It's nice when sexy naked people look at you. I am definitely on to something here. Many of them have sunglasses and many have open speechless mouths surrounded by chapped, spotted lips, and I think, they look hungry, maybe they will eat me. I consider that, and I decide yes, it's okay, they can eat me. I like to cook for strangers. And it's not the sexy women who I notice the most, although there is this one, goddamnit, I was just on an astral plane and now I'm thinking the most explicit thoughts about this woman, who's got olive cream skin and big lips and sunglasses and black hair done up in a crow's nest, and who has painted a sunrise on her navel, and there's a silvery round C with little silver balls on its serifs, piercing her navel, such that it appears symbolically that she has pierced the sun, and I wonder if that symbolism is intentional and what it means, and I want to ask her about it, only the thing I notice even more than her is that the guy next to her — next to her except for this skinny old guy who's also got no clothes on, but who has a cowboy hat and reflective sunglasses and a bandanna (red), holds a bottle of water and had more hair on him than most people wear clothing, but really next to *him* is this six-foot tall man, at least, unless the rest of them are dwarves, a man who is muscular and shaved and tan and has his head shaved and wears speedo-style swim goggles, and his dick is fully erect, and he's got some pieces of metal through his scrotum, which I wouldn't be able to see if he wasn't holding his dick in his hand, not really rubbing it up and down like maybe I would do if I were him and watching some really sexy event involving me, and not feeling the least bit ashamed about masturbating in public, but he's not masturbating, he's just holding it in his one hand, and he's biting the thumb knuckle of his other hand and his elbows are tucked near his sides even though it's not cold, not that I can tell, and I realize he looks really afraid. All of these people are looking very scared right now, and they're all looking either at me or at something near me. Am I scaring them? Am I scary?

Who am I anyway?

So I start to reconstruct some of my history, and this
time it's okay, really, it's not painful at all. I know my
name, my name is Charlie and I'm from San Rafael,
and I went to a private high school and got a good job
in San Francisco — I'm a Windows NT Administrator!
I live in San Francisco and it's really expensive but fun,
and my friends and I went to the Burning Man festival
in the Nevada desert this year, it's my first year, and it's
incredible, indescribable, and I was just out wandering
on the playa with some people, and we were looking at
this amazing thing, this gigantic fast-moving thing, on
the horizon. How to describe a bizarre thing in a
bizarre setting? I was talking to Tony, I'm sure he's
around here someplace, about how my mind had shut
down involuntarily and I was feeling hypnotized by
everything that wandered across my field of vision, this
huge party, this spectacle, and here came this gigantic,
this gigantic, thing, thing, I can't explain what it was
but it was tall and had streaming flags streaming off of
it, and it spat fire and waved its enormous tentacles
and billowed its huge sail, and a guy with a bullhorn
stood up on top of the shaking mast of it, clinging
heroically to several lines of rigging, yelling
unintelligibly as it came closer, moving very fast,
people I saw a few jump off of it as it picked up speed,
the galloping thing, and the man on top, tugging at
the ropes that were pulling him off his perch, as the
thing rocked and scrambled closer. He was naked too,
with sunglasses, and a bandanna, and in the distance I
could make out the barest metallic glint on the tip of

his penis, and I thought, gee, why do people do that?, but he held a megaphone and squawked into it, I couldn't make it out, just static squawking as it came closer and I was struggling to hear what the hell he had to say, this master of the indescribably bearing-down-upon-Tony-and-me-thing, as people I noticed began running around, is this part of the thing's thing? These gaily painted people yelling and leaping and falling off of and running in front of me and towards and away from me, as the indescribable thing, which now emitted loud disco music and had eye-stalks and signs painted on its sails reading "BEHOLD THE INDESCRIBABLE THING!" came speeding towards me, and the man in the megaphone shouted "Move! Move!" and everybody moved, and he moved, but I liked it right where I was, and as the indescribable thing came closer I knew it was coming to meet me, and I would get to know it better.

But now the indescribable thing has gone, and left me with its seed of perfect knowledge, and I know I've somehow been chosen, somehow been impregnated with the awareness of how it all works, and that the indescribable thing was God, and that I came to this desert on this day and stood right here and God Itself ran over me and broke both my legs and a fair amount, I am realizing, of the other parts of my body, and it feels wonderful ... The pain, it's not pain, it's just sensation, action, it's the feeling of life, it's the energy bound up in me somewhere, I feel the shape of my legs and I think "who needs legs, I've got God in my brain!" and as several people gather around me and start to try to bear me away someplace, the rest of the crowd starts shouting "Don't move him!" and a huge fat pale woman, who is also completely naked except for a cowboy hat and a backpack-carried advanced hydration system and a diving watch, screams as she shoves through the crowd, I'm an EMT! Stand back! I'm an EMT! And someone else tells her in the calmest and most gentle and clear voice, It's okay, everything's fine, just close your eyes, back away from the scene, sit down, find your center, relax, and the EMT will wear off in about five hours. But she stiff-arms him right into the dust and marches more or less right over two other people, and screams at the man who's behind me, holding the undersides of my arms with his hands, which seem to have a lot of blood and bits of wood and hemp twine on them and are a little bit uncomfortable — but I'm certainly not complaining — and he lets me go, gently, and everybody backs away into a respectful but dense little circle.

And she asks me if I can talk, and only then do I realize, no, actually, I cannot talk. So I shake my head no, but what I want to tell her is hey, hey please, don't scream at the nice naked people, they're just watching me do my thing. Yes, that's it. My thing. I'm a being-run-down-by-God artist, and this is the performance I brought with me to the desert here, to share with everybody. I'm trying to demonstrate to you all how important it is to go run out in front of huge indescribable things as they rush toward you, instead of running away. I am hear to teach you people. Please, relax.

She's taking my pulse, she's telling the crowd she needs some rags, some clothing to tear into strips. And all the naked people look sheepishly around them, and someone has a tiny nylon sash which she says is no help at all, and someone else has a red feather boa, and that's about it for the clothing options in the immediate vicinity. So she rips off my t-shirt — my orange hunting t-shirt with the reflective strips on it, that you can see from ten blocks away, which I actually did see once from ten blocks away, in a store window, and was able to reduce my speed and pull into the parking lot of the hunters' supply store and purchase it for twenty bucks, which was a lot of money at the time, years ago when I was unemployed, and then I realize that I'm actually kind of pissed off now. Who is this EMT-smoking weirdo who wants to destroy my favorite shirt, the one you can see from far away, that one I bought because I wanted to be struck by lightning, not that I felt like it really would improve my chances, but I just had this feeling that in my quest to be struck by lightning, I should get that shirt, and sure enough, wearing that very t-shirt, which is the only item of clothing I have that I actually bother to get dry-cleaned, that I was actually struck not by lightning, but by God, which is the same basic thing, and that this T-shirt was a valuable tool for human enlightenment, and how short-sighted and ignorant it was of her to want to rip it up and use it just to stem my bleeding.

I tried to say, I'm okay, let me bleed, but she kept going and I couldn't speak. She said Wiggle your toes, and I wiggled my toes, and she said, Can you hear me, wiggle your toes if you can hear me, so I wiggled them some more, and she said, Are you wiggling, and God she was irritating, I mean, I'm playing along here, but don't expect me to show much enthusiasm for this interruption of my trip. And then I realized: that it was over, and the feeling I had a moment ago wouldn't last, and now I was worrying about my shirt, and my bleeding and my toes, and Tony, who I still hadn't seen, and my bag, and my water bottle and everything was going to be a big drag from here on out. And I heard a helicopter, in the distance, then coming closer, and then a huge strong wind rose up and blew dust into my eyes, as the lady who was on EMT explained that they were going to take me to a hospital in Reno, and that I would be fine, when in fact I had been fine and now I was going to be in Reno instead ... but oh well. Say goodbye to God, I thought, and I began to cry a little as I noticed the feeling in my body was becoming a little too strong for my liking. And then some men came and put me on a thing, and the thing was carried over to the helicopter, and one more time I looked into the faces of a huge assembled throng of naked, silent, confused people whose eyes you couldn't ever see and who stuck metal bits into themselves, and I knew they were worried too.

And just before they shut the helicopter door and air-lifted me away from my dream, I saw on the corner of the clearing a huge mass of twisted rods, uncoiled ropes, fire retardant sprayed over smoking retarded fires, sashes, wires, engine oil, latex, steam, grass, sticks,

wood, cloth, and on one knee beside it was the man I
has seen who rode it on towards me, back when it was
whole, and I tried to wave to him, I wanted him to
come closer so I could thank him, but instead he
stayed there, bent and weeping over the wreck of the
indescribable thing.

DANGER!

In order to save you from yourself, we have labeled this
large red button. It reads: DO NOT PUSH. Please,
do not push the large red button. Every time you push
the button, someone you don't know who lives far
away will die, or maybe you will get some candy.
BUTTON WARNING! Don't push it. There will be
a bright flash and a loud noise, and the boredom you
are so goddamn sick of will vanish, replaced by
something graphic and life-altering and loud.
EXPLOSIVE DECOMPRESSION DANGER. If you
twist the red handle, everybody will be killed — and in
a fascinating way, too. They will all be extruded
through this tiny airplane window like so much human
pasta. There's no alarm on this red handle, and no
fail-safe. Is the handle hard to twist? Is it oiled
regularly, or does it stick? Don't find out. DANGER!
DO NOT LICK THE EXPOSED WIRES! We have
exposed them for you to look at. They're really very
pretty, don't you think? Look very closely. Bring your
tongue just a few inches shy of the blistering mark, but
DO NOT lick the exposed wires. Look at the shiny
wires, then at the bold, courageous sign. Which one
will you choose? It's a big decision.

SCHOOL CROSSING. You weren't even thinking
about it. Nope, you weren't even considering
straightening that knee and bearing down hard on the
accelerator. Thump. Thump. Oh no, not you. DO
NOT THINK WHAT WE KNOW YOU MUST BE
THINKING. Don't blame us for putting the thought
in your head. UNDER NO CIRCUMSTANCES
THROW THINGS FROM THE TOP OF THE

EMPIRE STATE BUILDING. They will only get lodged in someone's bloody brain. Isn't that interesting? You don't want to do such interesting, hideous, easy-to-do things. Do you?

You don't want to suffer SEVERE TIRE DAMAGE, do you? You wouldn't want to brave a RADIATION DANGER. You are FRAGILE. You have MOVING PARTS. Smoking will kill you, but SMOKING NEAR THE PUMPS *might* kill you. Care to test your luck? Please don't, even though you will probably live and it will show them just how brave you are.

HANGING FROM, PLAYING WITH OR USING THIS TOWEL DISPENSER IN A MANNER OTHER THAN AS ILLUSTRATED MAY CAUSE SEVERE INJURY OR DEATH. Got that? DEATH. Study the diagram carefully. One false move and you're snuffed! But what if you don't dry your hands? ELECTROCUTION HAZARD, that's what.

The world is a minefield. Mine is the voice that will guide you through. But you must obey. NO PARKING NORTH OF HERE. Everything is a trap. Everything is very dangerous, people don't realize that. CURB WHEELS. The tigers are gone, but there are toasters everywhere, with metal forks lying beside them. Christmas tree lights. Cars. NARROW BRIDGE. We have technology and power and raw materials. DO NOT INHALE. We can make you all the rope you ever wanted. Miles and miles of supple, brightly striated hemp rope, exceptionally strong.

DANGER: ROPE HAZARD. Enough rope to hang yourself, your family, Mom, Dad, the dog, your boss, all your ex-girlfriends, the President and the Vice-President and everybody who ever did anything to hurt you, and all your friends, and a million starving Africans who never got the chance to do anything to anybody you've ever even heard of. Please, don't do it. YOU HAVE BEEN WARNED. 👁

Pang

Hey! I am Pang. I planted those tulips. No, those
there, yes. This is my favorite month of the spring. So
far! Ha! Look at that color! Someday I think they
will create a perfectly blue tulip, and then my palette
will be complete. See that row, the breech of white
there in front, four or five young ones bowing. That's
a wave breaking on a gravel beach. Can you see it?
Stand here. Now? Ha! There's a red boat over there, a
sailboat. There's no tulip that looks like a sail, I know,
but see the red hull? See the yellow nest on the green
mast? It's calm out there, but deadly. All over here —
come, look — see these? Wreckage. This is Crete. I
sailed there myself. I was blown out to sea off the
Taiwan shore when I was nine or ten. The Greeks
found me, took me aboard. I'm a Greek sailor.
Chinese, I can't even say it anymore. "Sang," that's
mother. I never saw her again. She had a garden,
though, I'll never forget it. See these circles, they draw
a ring around this point. Over here — here is where
you stand. Anywhere is okay, but here is best. Here
the tulips salute you. Good morning, gentlemen ...
Look! Over there! That sonovabitch has to go. That's
not mine, how did that get in? Too small to save ...
here, have a flower. I have a pin, where ... ah. Hold
still. Please, it's for you. You see, I have too many!
Ha! Now you are a young bachelor — the Greek girls
won't leave you alone if you go to Crete. ◈

The Oranges of Mr. Shark

My friend the great white shark is poorly socialized.
He was born with the instincts of his ancestors, and his
motivations are to hunt, kill, and eat other creatures.
He is honest about this, and eloquent, but underneath
it all, he is a shark's shark. Other creatures don't trust
him. Even his family keeps him at a fin's length.

He might better be described as my acquaintance.
We drink coffee at the same café down by the shore,
the one where the waiters all wear striped pantaloons
and the drinks come in little cups shaped like dogs and
cats. We sip out coffee, and talk about this and that.
He is funny, well-spoken and always immaculately
dressed. Sometimes he is a bit forward.

"I'm very lonely," he confided one day. "I've tried to
find a companion. I've gone out to the nicest
restaurants with the nicest people, but it seems that
whenever things start to go well, and I begin to relax,
the whole killing and eating thing gets in the way. I
can't help it, it's just my nature." My friend the shark
frowned a huge, toothy frown. "I don't know what to
do," he said, and he sipped at a cat's head full of
mocha.

"Hmm," I said. "Gee. Well."

"I'm not a bad creature," he said, running his tongue
around the edge of the mug, "I'm just constantly
hungry." A modicum of saliva gathered on his lip.

"Gee," I said, as he looked at me with a hungry eye, "that's too bad."

"Anyway," he said, "one ought to look on the bright side of things. Today the weather is beautiful, and I'm going for a swim. Why don't you hop on in and join me?"

"No no," I said, "I don't really, umm, feel up to it."

"Oh well ... then I'll see you later," said the shark, as he dove into the water and swam away.

I told the story of the shark's troubles to my friend Phil. Phil considers himself something of a matchmaker, and claims that he is personally responsible for no less than ten marriages in this city, some lasting years.

"Listen," he said, running his long, thin fingers through his long, thin beard. "I know this lovely sack of oranges."

"A sack of oranges?" I asked.

"Yes," he said, "a five-pound bag. Maybe we should introduce them."

"Fix them up, you mean?"

"Well yes, to put it crudely. Acquaint them with one another."

"But ... what would they have to talk about?"

"They wouldn't have to," said Phil with a gleam in his glass eye. "You say your friend was born to eat things, yes? And a sack of oranges wants to be eaten."

I told him that struck me as an unrealistic priority.

"Not at all, it makes sense. It's part of the evolutionary strategy of a tree. The tree can't walk, but it knows how to make these delicious oranges. An animal eats an orange, and then it walks on. The seeds of the orange pass through the tubes of the animal, and are deposited miles away in a fresh mound of fertilizer. There another tree grows. In this way, trees see the world."

"That sounds very unromantic," I said. "And I don't know if Mr. Shark is looking for that kind of a commitment just yet. And orchards don't thrive in salt water, et cetera."

"Don't worry," said Phil. "She's seedless."

◎   ◎   ◎

I didn't see either Phil or Mr. Shark for about a month because I became unexpectedly rolled up in a romance of my own, a brief fling with this amazing pack of Dutch cigarettes I met at a party in the waffle house

146

district. It was a fun, sexy, shallow, cheap and expensive affair, which ended happily but finally when she boarded a plane for Omsk, there to narrate a trilingual documentary about poststructuralism in dikes. When next I sauntered down to the seaside café, I was still bubbling over with silly romantic notions. Mr. Shark, resplendent in a white tuxedo, sat at the piano and picked at a lonesome tune with an adroit, melancholy fin. The piano top was lined with a row of empty cat heads, a candelabra and a mostly-eaten tray of celery and hummus.

"Ciao, Señor Shark," I greeted him. "How are you this fine evening, when the sky is so full of luxurious stars?"

"I am as blue as the sky is dark," he sighed, "and as dark as it is blue. Listen, here is my new song:

> *Oh, the shark has*
> *pretty teeth, dear,*
> *And he keeps them*
> *to himself,*

> *If you meet him,*   *He is lonely,*
> *always greet him,*   *he is gentle,*
> *And inquire*   *He admires*
> *about his health.*   *the sea and sky.*

>   *If you date him,*
>   *he'll devour you,*
>   *Otherwise, he's*
>   *a swimmin' guy.*

An appreciative old man sitting nearby clapped politely, and my friend gave one of his distinctive little bows of thanks.

"I think I can turn your frown around, Mr. Shark. I know of a certain young lady with whom you really ought to spend some time."

"No, no, thank you but no. I had another fiasco two nights ago, and it's given me a lot to think about. I'm through with the singles scene."

"A fiasco? Another bad date?"

"Indeed. A lovely girl, Martha, a harp seal I met in Monterrey while I was exercising with some surfer friends. She was beautiful, smart, possessed of delicate and sensual fur and deep, haunting eyes. Involved in a number of progressive community programs. Played the sitar. I rescued her from a furrier and she insisted on making me dinner."

"So, what happened?"

The shark gazed aside in shame, and then he slowly rolled back his vast rubbery lips. Between rows of glinting teeth I spied a few reddened flecks of fur. His breath stank unmistakably of hats. I shuddered.

"Well ..." I remarked, "hmm."

"So you see — here, have a carrot stick. You see what always happens? I feel terrible about the whole thing. And I've given it a lot of thought ... and I've decided to become a vegetarian."

"A vegetarian — you? Will you still eat fish?"

"Oh yes, of course, and probably a little chicken. But that's it. I am resigned to a life of platonic solitude, comforted by the knowledge that I am easing the suffering of others." And although he was too poised and noble a character to show it, I knew his sadness was a deep and painful one.

"Listen ... hear me out. I think I know just the inauguration for your new life. I really think you should meet this sack of oranges I know."

"Oh no, please, don't let me ruin this as well."

"Hear me out! She's a sack of oranges, she's from Florida. A wonderful, warm personality, very sweet and caring. She's just moved here, and wants to meet people."

"Ah," my friend said. "I don't date unsightly women."

"No, really, she's drop-dead gorgeous! Voluptuous, loaded with curves! And I have a feeling she'd be very understanding about your, um, your condition."

Mr. Shark was quiet and thoughtful for a few moments. Then a nearby waiter tripped over his pantaloons and spilled a tray of glasses. After general applause, our conversation turned to other subjects and regained its usual levity. An hour later I knew I had him hooked.

◉   ◉   ◉

By that time, Phil had worked a similar line of salesmanship on the sack of oranges. Mr. Shark called her one evening, they chatted for a while and agreed to let us broker them a date. But on the scheduled evening of the introduction Phil developed a sudden previous engagement, so I became saddled with the job of picking up Ms. Oranges at her apartment in town and dropping her off with Mr. Shark at the café. As I rode through the park on my bicycle, I grew less and less comfortable with the whole project. Why do I always try to intervene in the lives of people I hardly know? If things turn out badly, will they both hold it against me?

I arrived at the apartment and knocked on the door. "Come on in," a soft voice called, "I'm just getting dressed." I crept in. A moment later she appeared in the hallway, lit from above by a fluorescent plant light.

She was drop-dead gorgeous. And voluptuous. And loaded with curves. She was wearing one of those orange plastic fish-net stretch bags, and it left nothing to the imagination.

Yes, she sure was a sack of oranges.

"How do I look?" she asked.

"Wow," I half-stammered, "you look great! Really ... great!"

"Oh, you're sweet," she said. For a sack of oranges she sure had a beautiful voice. I felt a small, not uncomfortable grumble in my colon.

"Can I get you something to eat?" she asked. "You look hungry."

She smiled in a way I've never before been smiled at by a sack of oranges.

"We should go," I said. And I tucked her in my backpack.

"Hee hee," she said, "that tickles!"

◉   ◉   ◉

"Mr. Shark, this is Ms. Oranges. Ms. Oranges, this is Mr. Shark." He was dressed to the nines, looking even more dapper and sophisticated that I had ever seen him before. He immediately charmed her with a mildly risque joke concerning relatives of his living in the Florida Keys. Laughing together, they skipped away on a wave almost before I could wish them a pleasant evening. I sat down, ordered a biscotti, congratulated myself and imagined the happy pair and the fabulous time they would have together. Then I pictured them at the conclusion of their date, and suddenly I lost my appetite.

⦿   ⦿   ⦿

I didn't go back to the café for a few weeks. I suppose I was avoiding Mr. Shark. I did however run into Phil at the laundromat-pizzeria near my apartment. He mentioned in an offhand way that he hadn't heard from his friend the sack of oranges recently.

I was incredulous. "Were you really expecting to?"

"Well, I haven't called her. I suppose she's been occupied with your friend the great white shark."

"Phil, think about it ..."

Phil thought about it. "You think he's eaten her?"

"Of course! Probably on the first date!"

"I really don't think she's that kind of girl."

"Does it matter? I mean ... I feel terrible. This was all your idea."

"Don't be hard on yourself," he said, taking a bite of pizza, "like I said, it's the way of things. A brief moment of ecstasy in this world is better than ending up as orange concentrate or something."

◉   ◉   ◉

Frustrated, I left Phil with his pizza and his dirty laundry and I walked all the way to the café. I didn't really expect to see Mr. Shark there so early in the day, and had no idea what I would say if I did. I just wanted to face the situation somehow.

As it turned out he was there, seated at a corner table, wearing sunglasses and sipping a glass of water. And he wasn't alone — he had a short, dumpy-looking and rather poorly dressed lamprey attached to his dorsal area.

"Meet Esmerelda," he said with a tired-sounding grimace, "my special one." Esmerelda stood up, smiled awkwardly and curtseyed as well as she could, and then returned to his side, where she made small sucking noises.

"Esmerelda's English skills aren't so good. I met her in the Caribbean during my recent vacation. We've become rather, well ... you can see." Esmerelda cooed, and stroked Mr. Shark's belly with her brown-grey finless tail.

He leaned closer to me and whispered, "I know what you're probably thinking: she's coarse. She's vulgar. I deserve better. But you know, I feel this tremendous sense of relief, just to be in a simple straightforward relationship like this, with everything out in the open. Plus, she's a great dancer and a fabulous cook! And I really think we have something that will last, which is what I've always wanted but could never find." He patted her tail affectionately, and winced slightly as she nipped him. "And you know, if it doesn't work out, I'll dump her. She has no passport." He winked, then winced again.

I was speechless. A pantalooned waiter brought me my usual treble mocha, but I waved it away.

"So you're no longer a *vegetarian*, then?" I finally said.

"Ah," he said, and sighed, "well, you know, I'm sorry things didn't work out with your friend. I guess she told you all about my sudden departure. I was inexcusably rude. Please, if you get the chance, tell her I'm sorry. She's a wonderful girl, I just ... I had a lot on my mind that night. I guess I had a bit too much to drink. As you can see, I'm on the wagon." He dipped a fin in his glass of water and touched it to his enormous tongue. "Horrible stuff, really. Fish procreate in it. But it's doing me a lot of good."

Esmerelda came up for air at that point, whispered something foreign in Mr. Shark's ear, and ran a raspy tongue along his left gill. She smiled at me, and winked. Mr. Shark blushed beet red.

"I won't tell you what she just proposed, but I assure you it was a compliment. I think, ah ... I think we'll be heading home for lunch now. Nice to see you, as always. We'll meet again soon, I'm sure. Come along, darling."

Mr. Shark waddled awkwardly to the shore with his new companion, and vanished into the ocean.

◉   ◉   ◉

I went home and called Phil to get Ms. Oranges' phone number, but he was out. So I put on a nice shirt, collected my bicycle and rode over to her apartment. It was about four o'clock in the afternoon when I arrived, locked my bike and climbed the steps to her door. I brought along some paper and a pen to leave a note, but when I rang the bell, she answered. This time she was wearing a little burlap slip and holding a screwdriver.

"Why hello!" she said. "I wasn't sure if I'd see you again. C'mon in and help me change this lightbulb in the bedroom."

I followed her. "Hi, I'm sorry I didn't call ahead, I, um, lost your number."

"Oh, don't worry about it!" She took my pen and paper, scribbled down a number, tore off the sheet and folded it into my hand. "Don't lose it again. Now, you're a tall guy; why don't you screw this in while I go fix us some juice?"

I changed the lightbulb easily enough, and returned to the kitchen. "I just saw my friend Mr. Shark," I said. "I'm sorry to hear ... I mean, I was worried ... um, how did that all go?"

She tittered, and handed me a tall glass of orange juice. "Here, come sit down. Your friend is very nice, but I think he's afraid of women. Poor thing."

I laughed as we sat down together on her very narrow couch. "Afraid of women? I find that pretty hard to believe. Mr. Shark is nothing if not a lady-killer. In fact, I just sort of assumed that he ... um ..."

She frowned. "That he um? You say 'um' a lot."

"Well, let's just say I'm happy to see you intact."

"Intact."

"Well, I'm glad you weren't devoured."

"Hmph!" she humphed. "I'm not."

I blushed. A moment later we both started laughing.

We sat there together for a minute, smiling, looking silently at one another. I swallowed a mouthful of saliva. She was one hell of a sack of oranges, even more so with the afternoon sun shining through the window, highlighting her stippled skin. She leaned closer.

"Are you hungry?" she asked.

"I'm famished."

She gazed into my eyes searchingly. "Are you getting enough Vitamin C?"

"They say you can't get too much."

"They're right," she said, as she took my hand and squeezed it. "C'mon, let's go look at that light bulb."

Love Letter For The Apocalypse

Tall things are taller than shorter things. That's what
tall means. I am taller in my mind than a mental
dwarf, but a physical dwarf is also taller than me.
However, a building is also shorter than a dwarf's
mental mind, is the difference. If there are ten apples
in a basket and I hit you in the face with a dwarf, how
many baskets are left? To put it another way, the world
is composed of like energy man, and it's all like
flowing, and love makes it go around, so relax and have
sex with me. No, here, smoke this first, then relax,
then have sex with me. I mean ... to put it another
way, this is a stickup. I have a gun. Please do not step
on the silent alarm. Please put all of the bananas in a
disposable plastic bag. No I do not want a reusable
hemp bag. I want a disposable plastic bag. I am a
criminal, a bad person. Now please, the grapefruit and
all of the oranges. And the organic Swiss chard.
Hurry! Okay, now everybody lie face down on the
floor. I'm sorry if it's gross — it's your organic food
co-op, you should vacuum more often or scrape it or
something. Now, I want you to say Ommmmm three
hundred times. I'll leave my astral projection here to
keep guard on you people while my corporeal form
collapses into the getaway rickshaw outside, so no
funny stuff. No clever remarks. No witty, insightful
comments. I want to see no hand-puppetry, no mime,
no silly facial expression or impersonations of
well-known figures. No cartooning! I hear one
knock-knock joke out of you and I'll blow you to
smithereens. Do you understand? If you understand,
signify your consent to these legally binding conditions
by remaining perfectly still and saying Ommmmmm.

Very good. Now I want you all to know that because you have signalled your consent, this is no longer a robbery but a voluntary transaction, so the police can't help you. Don't even try to call them. Okay? Bye. Or to put it another way: if you were a mountain and I was a tunnel, and my feelings for your were flatbed cargo cars loaded with construction materials, and on the other side of you our future together was a large clear-cut area of federal forest, and the feelings you have for me were the three black helicopters hovering over the locomotive threateningly, and my heart was a weasel and your soul was a colony of bacteria and the cargo cars of my feelings collided with the helicopters of your feelings inside of my tunnel through your mountain, and together all of this emotion spilled out onto the clearcut of our future and exploded in a fireball of love, and my heart and your soul were both engulfed in flame, still I think I would rather have that then what I have now, where your heart is like a thoroughly modern Pitney Bowes office postal meter that can only be refilled with love by calling a toll-free 800 number and exchanging mysterious codes with a computer voice on the other side, and I feel like a care package that's poorly wrapped inside an envelope that's too thick for your auto-feed slot, and all I want is to feel your hard kiss and your rollers whisking me into the OUT basket, but I am too fat and instead I sit in the bottom of the IN basket and none of the Kelly Girls have enough initiative to even spit on me and apply stamps, and anyway I don't want their stamps I only want the beautiful, crisp cancellation that only you can give. That's approximately how I feel. Since you asked. And if you think I'm sick or fat or weird or I don't make much sense or I'm harassing you, sexually, and making the workplace inappropriate for cogitation, well, I'm sorry, but I am what I am and what I am is, is what I'm trying to say is, is this: I ... quote L-word unquote ... you. That's what I'm trying to say. 👁

The Great Mechanico
(vs. the Liberal Media)

Now I have invented the cellular remote control. I, the great MECHANICO, have freed home entertainment system owners from the geographic boundaries that once fettered them.

I have perfected the edible murder weapon, the self-upholstering chair, and the recursive noodle that drove famine from Italy. I have walked on water with my poly-fiber aquawalkassins. I have isolated the DNA strand that determines golf skill.

My mighty semiparallel superconducting number cruncher has reduced the digits of ε to a powder too fine to probe even with my astounding Scanning Tunneling Wiggling Stapling Proton Pneumatiscope. I, the great MECHANICO, have done all this.

To say that my enemies and detractors cower when my name is mentioned would be, perhaps, an understatement. To state that beautiful and surprisingly intelligent women's hearts explode with passion as I pass would be, perhaps, an exaggeration — and yet, my CPR skills are well-practiced. To suggest that mine is the most brilliant mind that ever made a home within a man would be uncharacteristically immodest; but obversely, to argue with the conclusions of the Oregon Center for Advanced Cognitive Appreciation, MENSA's National Star Search program, and the other-worldly advice of the President's outer space liaison, that would be foolhardy. And I am no hardy fool.

I was asked by certain Los Angelean interests to invent a plot-sucking gun, that might extract the basic premise of a book or manuscript from a distant vantage point. Although I had already conceived such a device, I sensed that these men would use my gifts to gain ill-gottenly, and I dismissed them. The great MECHANICO has lots of offers coming in; his agent screens heavily.

Dusk: it weighs on the soul of the great MECHANICO. He reaches into the vast folds of his cranium to pluck a suitably maudlin metaphor. In dusk, he decides, the papadum of the MECHANICO soul drowns beneath the ghee of mortal expectation.

No; something occidental would be more appropriate. In dusk, the MECHANICO soul is suffused in the pitch of societal responsibility, and blackened.

No, that's not it either. MECHANICO knows, the subtlety of language is the most elusive butterfly the collector of nuance might ever hope to ... to ... oh damn. Damn damn damn. Never mind. Enough poetry. Dusk is ended. MECHANICO has more important knots to loosen.

Today is a great day — MECHANICO releases to the public his Quantum Ossification Engine (which temporarily fossilizes a fleeing miscreant or would-be attacker), his Stereolithographic Convection Oven (which carves meat and poultry while baking, following laws of proportion and division laid down in

Renaissance times), and, perhaps most importantly, the Anti-Arthritic Mitten.

However, at the press conference, he is assailed with questions. Does the Quantum Ossifier violate the Geneva Convention? Does the Stereolithographic Oven pose a threat to children? Are the mittens available in other colors?

MECHANICO heaves a sigh. No, no, no to all your questions. You are bestowed a great gift, the fruit of my genius, the offspring of my labors. How can you question the goodness of these things? What more do you want?

The onslaught continues:
— MECHANICO, is there truth to the rumor?
— No truth to the rumor, no.
— Are allegations concerning this and that false?
— Yes, decidedly.
— Can you either confirm or deny at this time?
— No.
— What is your connection with the secret government project?
— MECHANICO cannot answer, it's a secret.
— If a murderer chokes to death on the edible murder weapon, what is your moral reaction?
— MECHANICO considers this cosmic justice.
— MECHANICO, are you a homosexual pederastic necrophile?
— No.
— Are you perhaps a deviant masochistic cophargist?

— No.

— A pot-abusing philanderer?

— No. What is the point of these questions?

— MECHANICO, does the world truly require a cellular remote control?

— The marketplace will decide this, not I.

— MECHANICO, what do you say to those who hark back to a simpler era?

— I encourage this harking. I ... MECHANICO believes that harking is a perfectly natural and healthy human behavior, and nothing to be ashamed about. However, it is well known that excessive, constant harking can leave one blinded to the possibilities of the future. The desire to hark can be moderated through daily exercise, frequent showers, and regular doses of scientific determinism. MECHANICO would be glad to suggest study materials that might —

— MECHANICO, you are missing the point. Technological advancement has been its own primary justification since the age of the Greeks. Today we are inundated with strange new inventions, some of obvious import, some of dubious merit, and many that clearly serve only destructive ends. Scientists frequently lend their scientific power to anyone who will fund their research. In this way they not only perpetuate the socioeconomic class system of which they frequently predict the extinction (due to the imminence of free electricity, plentiful food, an end to all disease, et cetera), but in many cases allow profiteers to restrict the usefulness of breakthroughs that could potentially benefit all of humankind. Meanwhile the ever-quickening pace of social change brought on by new technology produces a widely-recognized alienation and uncertainty about the future, even in the very young. Shouldn't scientists and inventors begin to take responsibility for the unpredictable waves of change that they launch across the world? Isn't it the merest ethical duty of a scientist, before allowing an invention or a technology or a technique to be used by others, to secure some guarantee that A: their work will not be used in the creation or refinement of weapons of death and destruction, and B: that the social necessity of their work will not be used to profit at the expense of the poor and/or truly needy?

— Sir, MECHANICO does not get involved in politics. Good day. ☜

The Talking Bottle of Gin

A man met me in the street and said: Come see my
talking bottle of gin. We went to his small, sparse
apartment beneath a mosque in the center of town.
From beneath his bed he produced a valise, and from
the valise two tumblers and a bag, and from the bag,
the gin.

It looked like a regular bottle of Tanqueray, poorly
kept, with the seal missing and the label torn.

He poured himself a glass, and one for me. We drank.
"Listen," he said. I thought to myself: oh the things
I'll do for a bottle of gin. We had another drink.
"Listen," it said, but I didn't hear anything. He poured
me another drink, and so did I.

The gin bottle said a few words on the impossibility of
sainthood. "Amen," I said, and I had another drink.
My host had another drink as well.

The gin lost its initial shyness. It regaled us with
off-color humor. It sang a brief medley of
anti-prohibition songs of the 1920s. It analyzed my
dreams. We talked a little bit about Kennedy, but we
disagreed. I had another.

I had another. The bottle of gin began to slur its
speech, and occasionally it misplaced possessive
pronouns. It introduced a long tale about something
awful it did once, when it was young. It rambled on
and off the subject of its deepest fears. It made me a
little uncomfortable. I had another drink.

168

The talking bottle of gin didn't sound at all well. As the night eroded it told me embarrassing things. It confessed a belief in racial theories. It swore an oath of loyalty to our eternal friendship, and when we refused to do the same, it began to curse and tremble. I guess the talking bottle of gin knew what we were thinking.

My host suggested we polish off the bottle.

The talking bottle of gin made a wild, staggering plea for mercy. In the name of the virgin. In the name of the saints. In the name of decency. For the sake of future gin drinkers. It never sobered, but as it sputtered it began to glow and shake, and gradually it entered a state of glossolalia, sputtering in non-existent tongues as if possessed by ancient spirits. It was an astounding thing to watch.

Its unconstructed effusion drained from a wild pitch to a trickle. We killed the bottle and that was that. ◉

Magic Trick with Dog and Stick

Okay, this is a stick. You hold it in your hand like this. No, like ... right, like that. Now here is a dog. We'll start you with a small one. The way this works is ... no no, don't touch the dog, not yet, listen, here, this is how it's going to work: when I give the signal, you throw the stick as far as you can, see, out that way into that meadow of sticks and grass and mud and water. Understand me so far? You, throw, stick? Okay? Good. Now, at the same moment that you throw the stick that way, I'm going to throw this dog the other way, out into that busy intersection there. See? Then the stick and the dog will turn around and — yes? Sorry, was there a question? Yes? You there, with the tie. Why do I ... oh well, you know. I guess just to keep things fair. You know, you throw something, I throw something ... anyway it's the rules. Let's just try this out a few times and see how it goes before we start finding faults in the system, shall we? Okay! So, then the stick and the dog will turn around and run back towards each other, and that's when ... you sir, what's your name? Okay, you take this bag DON'T OPEN IT SIR! Please, not yet, not until the moment when the stick and the dog both turn around, and that's when, not a moment sooner sir, that's when you release the venomous asps! Sir? Sir, you dropped the asps. Sir ... okay, how about you there. C'mere sir, now, take this bag, don't be afraid there's nothing to fear, just take this bag, very good, and at the moment I just described, you pull on this drawstring to open the bag, and then drop it on the ground right ... here. I'll make an X with my shoe. See that? Good. Yes, then you can run away. If you can, sir, try to run that way, towards that car. That's where I'll be, as soon as I throw the dog.

Yes, yes sir? Um ... sir? Hang ... hang on a second sir. Sir? Listen. Hey! Listen! I am a professional circus freak, and Bowser here is a veteran of over one hundred such stunts, and I assure you I would not be up here, today, doing this trick for your benefit, for your amusement, if I thought there was any risk of injury or harm to this dog. Why I've know Barky here all his, all her life. Fixed her myself. Please folks, just trust me. I won't steer you wrong. Now, I need two people, you there, and you? Ma'am? Yes, come right on up here, no danger, now, you put this black wire in your mouth. Okay? Thank you. And you sir, put this red wire in your mouth. Okay? Bite down a little? Thanks. Now, the two of you should under no circumstances touch each other until I give the signal. What's going to happen is, the dog is going to run out of traffic, back towards the stick, and the stick is going to be chased by the asps, and they're all going to run towards that fence over there, which as you can see if you look over at that set of equipment over there, yes folks, this is an electrified fence. Now, I need one more volunteer to operate the garden hose. Any takers? Anybody? I can't do it myself, I'm throwing the dog. You sir, can you ... a question. Ah. I see. You have a question. Okay, please sir, tell me, what is your question this time? Yes? Hmm. How does the stick run? That's your question: How Does The Stick Run? Okay here's your answer sir: IT'S A FUCKING MAGIC TRICK ISN'T IT? Now would you SHUT

171

FUCKING UP and take this HOSE here and DO what I SAY or do I have to throw this DOG at you? Hey! Come back here! You, buddy, asp guy, go tell that guy to come back here. Hey wait! Don't drop those snakes, they're sensitive! Hey lady, who said you could take that wire out? Oh come on! We're almost ready to start? Don't you people care about magic? How can you disappoint such a cute little doggie? Look! Cute little doggie! Come Back! Please! Cute happy doggie wants to play with you! Hey! Come back here! Hey! 👁

ADVERTISEMENT

Due to restrictions that are largely legal rather than ethical, we cannot promise that spending your hard-won dollars on our MSL products will in any way improve or enhance the quality of your life, your health, or your financial fortitude. It does in fact seem that spending your hard-won dollars on frivolous entertainment crap such as we sell will do the exact opposite of at least one of those things. However, we can and will say this: that MSL products are GUARANTEED FOR LIFE, whatever that means, and that MSL products are 73% MORE GREASE-LIFTING or STYLE-CONSCIOUS or something than some other thing, measured in some way that we will insinuate is meaningful, so that maybe you will think that we stand behind our products, or that we employ some team of scientists who are able to measure units of grease-liftingness in their test tubes and therefore able to magic-scientifically enhance our products in some way that you don't at all understand but still believe to be good and important. If you are the type of person who falls for this sort of thing — really, we are constantly amazed how many of you there are — then it is likely that we will end up with some of your money. So of course, yeah, we'll say that. We'll say anything. We also can and will insert normal human grunting noises like YO! and UH-HUH! and BABY! and MMMM! into our advertisements such that maybe some time soon when you're not consuming entertainment and your bullshit detector is off-line and your shields are down, you'll grunt in one of these normal human ways and simultaneously be reminded of this very MSL advertisement, but probably not remember why exactly, and maybe you will confuse this unbidden leaping-into-your-mind of our advertisement, this conditioned response that we are teaching you, MMMM!, maybe you will confuse this with some deep inner desire or interest of your own, that you don't fully understand but hope will maybe cheer you up if you act upon it. If you don't know yourself enough to tell the difference between your own ideas and desires and the ones we plant in you — and who does know themselves that well, really — then the odds are good that you will mistakenly give us some more of your money. Ha ha. We also can, and will, simply command you to: ORDER NOW!, to BUY TODAY!, to DON'T DELAY!, to just DO IT!, because some of you out there are actually pretty suggestible, we've found, you are either really gullible or not completely well in the head — it's amazing how many of you there are — and these voices that shout at you from the advertising stream seem real and compelling and somewhat threatening, and therefore you will actually BUY TODAY! either out of terror of psychic retribution or simply because somewhere along the line you learned to follow orders. And so some more of your money will be ours. We win, you lose. Also, we can and will introduce slogans, totally meaningless but strangely memorable statements such as: MSL: MANUFACTURED WITH PRIDE BY AMERICANS WHO CARE, or: MSL: BECAUSE IT'S SOME STUFF, or SWIM LARGE WITH MSL, and even if almost all of these slogans seem really stupid and pointless to you — they sure do seem that way to us — still someday one of them will resonate idiosyncratically with the trivia in your mental attic, and boom, we're in there, MSL, and from then on you will smile and chuckle when you hear the slogan repeated in any of our many, many advertisements, and you will decide that down there at MSL there must be at least one person who is like you, and who isn't all bad. Which just isn't true. We are not like you, and we are all bad, and we spend all day in our nice offices eating really nice food and thinking up newer, cleverer ways of lying to you, confusing you, occupying your thoughts and the space between your thoughts, cultivating in you obsession with us, distracting you from seeing what we're doing, controlling you and taking away all your money. Because that's what advertising is. And we're really, really good at it. We're so good at it that we're even telling you all about how we do it because we know that there is a market segment of you, large and getting larger, that is trying to defend itself against our onslaught, and that a common defense mechanism you are trying to use is to reject, disbelieve and distrust any and all advertisements, to do the very opposite as much as possible and, paradoxically, to satisfy your deep human longing to trust others while playing out your contrarian strategy by embracing only those advertisements which boldly state: HERE IS A WHOLE PILE OF BAREFACED FLAT FUCKING EVIL STINKING LIES FROM MSL for you to make a game of pretending not to believe while believing, trusting, and obeying, so as to ameliorate the cruel knowledge that we have penetrated your feeble defense mechanism, you cannot escape, we still control you.

So: BUY THE DAMN MSL CATALOG. Fill out the form. Send it to us, with the self-addressed stamped envelope and the money. Send it to:

MSL THOUGHT CONTROL PROJECT
5536 NE 27TH AVE
PORTLAND, OR 97211-6230

Don't forget to send the money.

EYEHEART PERSONALS —
for the discriminating and lonely.

"AFTER I RAN MY AD IN EYEHEART, hundreds of strange men called me at home!" Call 431-6746 to place an ad.

ARE YOU EXPERIENCED? I'm not! SF 20-32, Jewish preferred, seeks same for etc.

ARE YOU SCRAWNY? Skinny? Weak? Austrian bodybuilder will taunt you severely. Arnold, box 11.

BAD PERSON SOUGHT by disciplinarian. Box 794. Please, no regrets.

BLONDE, WF, 24, brain surgeon, fluent in seven languages, seeks philosopher, 30-35, charming, insightful, sensitive, blonde. Respond to Shauna, Box 3607. Please, blondes only.

CUCUMBERS ARE SEXY but they can't buy you lingerie. Men are hairy, but they fart in bed. What to do? Lonely AF seeks hunk to exploit, make fun of. Box 2399

DANCING THE TANGO, MADRAS cuisine, laughing at Conan O'Brien, drinking chicken soup through a straw — why do people do these things? 3578

DENTAL STUDENT SEEKS masochist for help with upcoming exams. $$$. Call Paul, box 3722

DESPERATELY LONELY, no friends, please talk me out of ending my pathetic life, especially if you are a SJF, physically fit, 23-27, a good listener, tall, have curly hair, like classical music, can appreciate sports and fine beers, enjoy housework, cooking, sexually voracious. Don, box 1107. Pls. incl. photo.

DISCIPLINE NEEDED by lazy, unproductive office workers. MBA preferred. Box 3722

DISCIPLINE SOUGHT by unruly teen. Detention, grounding, suspension of allowance OK. No counseling! Greg, Box 1963.

DO YOU LIKE LONG walks, long talks, tall tales, big ideas, stiff competition, etc? Contact box 1017 for lengthy discussion.

DULL WM SEEKS INTERESTING, busty blond for topical fun. Contact box 3440

FORMER BLONDE, 45, GWM, seeks still-blonde GWM, 30-35, for transplants, dancing. Harold. Box 2954.

HOT BLONDE, 7, seeks wealthy, sophisticated older gentleman (10-12) for swings, ice cream, long walks, possible doctor. Include photo, pager number. Box 8821.

HUNGRY FOR LOVE? SWMC seeks SWFC for dinner, breakfast, maybe lunch. Respond box 2105.

I AM GOOD WITH CHILDREN. Please let me be good with yours. Buddy's Day Care. See "Business Opportunities" next section. Oh boy!

I AM INCREDIBLY UGLY — photos available $5. send to Rudy, c/o Personals, or box 4364

I HAVE BEEN TRULY NAUGHTY, but I feel no remorse. Please help — box 2341.

I LOVE TO BE SAT ON by fat naked ladies. Otherwise I am pretty normal. Serious responses only to Box 2993.

"I MET THE MAN OF MY DREAMS in EYEHEART personals — I can no longer escape him by waking up!" Call 431-6746 to place an ad.

KNOCKOUT REDHEAD, 27, full figure, seeks generous, mature companion for money only. Brenda, Box 2400. Please include photo, $20 application fee.

LONG WALKS? I'M GAME! Fit AM, 27, seeks asphalt, spaniel, you. Box 1233, please include shoe size.

LONG WALKS — romantic? or compulsive? Informative videotape explains all! Cult Awareness Associates, Box 1709.

LONG WALKS sought by long-legged SF, 24. Stamina a must! Respond to box 2828.

LONG WALKS — why ask why? George, 3318.

MASOCHIST, 41, seeks sharp/hot objects for hurting self. Please forward to box 3688.

MASOCHIST seeks anaesthesiologist for experimental relationship. I will go deep if you will go slow. Alan, Box 1967

MASOCHIST seeks dental assistant or chiropractor for serious relationship. Massage therapists need not apply. Marge, Box 3091.

MASOCHIST sought by acupuncture student. Mutual arrangement, possible renum. Cy, Box 2772

NO WALK TOO LONG for this rugged 45-year-old BM. Can you keep up? Chad, Box 2424.

OH GOD YES OH GOD — Christian SWM seeks non-smoking WF, 30-45, busty, for platonic friendship only. Christ is the answer — are you the question? 4090, please include photo.

ONANISTS NEEDED — undergraduate thesis project — no payment, but possible TV appearance. Contact Brian at box 2282

ONANISTS REQUIRED by large marketing firm. You could be a star! Respond box 991

ONANISTS SOUGHT for major motion picture. Send portfolio with photo to Box 2988 for more information.

ONANISM — IS IT FOR you? Illustrated booklet reveals little-known facts. Send VISA/MC with exp. date to box 3077.

ONE-LEGGED 6'3" ALBINO male sports writer, Latvian, seeks same. 1004. Serious please.

ONE-OF-A-KIND GUY seeks 1-of-a-kind gal for 1-of-a-kind fun. Respond to Dave, Box 3381

ONE-OF-A-KIND GUY seeks 1-of-a-kind gal for 1-of-a-kind fun. Respond to Mike, Box 2390

ONE-OF-A-KIND GUY seeks 1-of-a-kind gal for 1-of-a-kind fun. Respond to Steve, Box 4029

ONE-OF-A-KIND, WF, 33, seeks intelligent, handsome WM artist, 25-35, for long walks, moonlight, the usual. Elaine. 3423.

SAFE SEX — GET PAID! Men! Eager ladies in your area will pay you for intimate services. Illegal? Degrading? One way to find out! Box 1779

SUBMISSIVE AM, 23, seeks submissive W/BF, 20-25, for clingy, codependent relationship. You call me — EYEHEART Box 2117

SUBMISSIVE WM, 35, seeks pain, injury, possible death at hands of WF 20-25, busty. Box 1104 for more info.

TWO BUSTY BLONDES sought by slob. Sex, possible cook/clean. Bruce — box 1918

UNIQUE INDIVIDUAL: WF, 32, one of a kind, seeks arty hunk for whirlwind romance. Laura, Box 2931

UNIQUE INDIVIDUAL, WF, 34, seeks hunky artist for fast times & fun. Loni, Box 1019

UNIQUE, INTERESTING WM, 29, seeks gorgeous intellectual WF, 20-30, for intellectual & erotic pursuits. Respond to Mike, Box 309

UNABLE TO SUPPRESS my strange craving for long walks. Please help! Karen, box 3883.

WEALTHY BLONDE seeks busty older man for mutual arrangement. Please respond to 2900

WEALTHY, MATURE, SPIRITUAL W/M, 57, looking for an affectionate companion to share good times, shower with adoration and gifts. Must be a good listener. Please send photo to Box 2388, John.

WEALTHY OLDER MAN seeks usual. Enrico, Box 2114.

WILL WORK FOR FOOD — please send job
descriptions, food photo to Gus, EYEHEART Box
4661

X-RAY TECHNICIAN seeks masochist for
experimental art project. Tattoos OK. Box 1663

X-RAY TECHNICIAN sought by curious, trusting
masochist. No long walks! Nina, Box 1849

YOU: HOMELESS BM, 45-50, blue jacket, at park
bench downtown. Me: handsome WM, 27, lawyer at
prestigious firm, brown hair, blue eyes. Give me back
my briefcase or I will sue! Larry, Box 2101 👁

Fitness Goddess Grace Grimes
(read this one aloud)

Fitness Goddess Grace Grimes.
Fitness Goddess Grace Grimes.
Fitness Goddess Grace Grimes.
Fitness Goddess Grace Grimes.
Goodness Fatness Grace Groans.
Fatness Goodness Grease Grimes.
Gibbous Fibbous Gribb Globb.
Oootness Oddness Arse Arms.
Arse Arms Gobness Flabness.
Fartness Fatness Gobs Glum.
Fibness Flobness Garp Goo.
Arbness Ibness Oof Arf.
Fitnit Gobgib Grass Groans.
Goodness Godness Garf Glines.

Nicholas was reading the paper, back to front, the dangerous way, and he found the place where you send in the form to win either a) a free six-month membership in an exercise apparatus holding company or b) a free 1999 Aerobics & Fitness Calendar featuring full-page spreads of Fitness Goddess Grace Grimes. Fitness Goddess Grace Grimes, I asked? Yes, he replied, Fitness Goddess Grace Grimes, of www.gracegrimes.com, who is apparently a Fitness Goddess, which is a job description I didn't know existed. The title Fitness Goddess means something a bit less than Porn Star, but a bit more than Aerobics Instructor. You can buy photographs and videotapes of Fitness Goddess Grace Grimes, in her revealing Fitness Goddess Outfit. They may improve your circulation, they may not. Or you can fill out the form to win the 1999 Aerobics & Fitness Calendar. Or you can just do what we do, and simply say her name over and over until you reach The Zone:

Fitness Goddess Grace Grimes.
Fitness Goddess Grace Grimes.
*Fitness Goddess Grace Grimes versus Business Goddess
        Kate Kleen.*
*Business Goddess Kate Kleen versus Bigness Goddess
        Bruce Brine.*
*Bigness goddess Bruce Brine versus Ignatz Podless
        Grease Jones.*
*Ignatz Podless Grease Jones versus 1998 Mr. Leather
        of Washington.*
*1998 Mr. Leather of Washington versus the Clark County
        Boy Scout Choir.*
*The Clark County Boy Scout Choir versus Two Dozen
        Muscular Shaved Greased Men.*
*Two Dozen Muscular Shaved Greased Men versus
        Sixteen Asexual Fleshy Globs.*
*Sixteen Asexual Fleshy Globs versus Fitness Goddess
        Grace Grimes.* ☜

The Man Who Was Born Typing

Once there was a man who was born typing. It wasn't easy on his mother, let me tell you, and the labor lasted thirty hours. Then out he popped, knibbling at the knobbles of a tiny bone-and-gristle Smith-Corona, and the placental sac was littered with tiny typed sheets of clear tissue. The doctors threw the sac away, but that was all right, because he kept on typing.

He kept typing as he teethed, as he suckled, through the acquisition of language, through the discovery of sex, he kept on typing, typing, typing, and when anybody ever asked him what he was typing he would reply "the story of my life." By the time he was ten he had filled his family's garage with neatly stacked pillars of typewritten pages. By the time he was fifteen they had to move to a larger house.

The man who always typed was too busy typing to spend time stuffing envelopes, filling out SASEs, reading rejection slips, so nobody published his work, and those friends and acquaintances who did read it found it interesting, but very weird and disorganized, and once or twice they even offered to help him with the organizing and the editing. But he wasn't interested in re-typing, just typing, so he kept on typing and the stacks rose higher.

He went to college, where he wrote a lot of essays, and did well, and got into grad school and continued to type. The university published whatever he wrote, without really reading it, and they gloated over the volume of their chopped and bound output, so they kept him on. They wanted him to give lectures but he had no interest, so he'd go to the lecture hall, stand at the lectern and type, and then hand the sheets to a grad student who would read them out loud.

And eventually through sheer force of volume he got famous, a little, and some people decided they liked what he wrote, although they didn't understand it, not at all, still, it was exotic. So they gave him tenure and an office, and young grad students would occasionally get sexually fixated on him and give him blowjobs as he typed, and he enjoyed them, but not enough to stop typing. And the consensus among those who knew him was that he was cold, distant, he never stopped typing when he talked to you and he never looked at you, even though he was an accomplished touch-typist. He'd just stare into the space in front of him, chin slightly raised, lips pursed in an expression of ecstasy. He was handsome really, but cold, and he had no friends except his bone-and-gristle Smith-Corona, his deformed twin. All day long he talked to it, and it talked back, and the clattering of its keys was like the chattering of old teeth.

The man who always typed had one stack of papers he handed to the university, to publish as they saw fit or do whatever they liked, as per their agreement with him. But he had another stack, the secret stack, which was for him alone, him and his twin. People could tell when he was working on the secret stack because his visage would lose its calm and become inflamed, excited, emotional and insane, and he would scream and whoop and weep and wail as he typed. But what he wrote nobody knew. He locked the pages away in a secret location.

A cult formed, of people who supposed they knew what the secret stack contained. His public works, his official oeuvre, was so strange and convoluted, so chaotic — what could this secret work contain? Some thought it was the novel, his first real complete novel. Others said it was the key, the great philosophical index that would let the rest of his work make sense and not seem so weird. And others said they had looked over his shoulder and seen one word, just one, repeated over and over and over. They said he was mad, insane, a crank, getting worse all the time. But he would not confirm or deny such statements, and the only thing he ever said, when asked what the secret stack contained, was "the story of my life."

Then people started to get interested in the story of his life, his background, his history, to get a hint at what made him so strange, and at what the secret papers might contain. Biographers went to his hometown and interviewed everybody, and came to the conclusion that he had been born with a bizarre appendage, and that his constant typing had by all means strained his relationship with his parents and with society, and that he had become an odd fish, stunted, socially inept, but that there was no root cause of anything he did or anything about him other than the fact that he was always typing, always always typing typing typing, and that he had been born that way.

He grew older, and as he did a lifetime's typing began to take its toll on him. At only forty years of age his hands became knurled with arthritis and his posture seemed very much to collapse, and it was not uncommon to see him resting his head on the top panel of his typewriter as he worked, leaning on it for support as the rest of his body withered. And the typewriter, too, grew thin and difficult, typed more slowly, broke its L key, forcing him to use the number 1 instead. And the sound of his typing seemed to grow difficult, filled more and more with typos, jammed keys, backspaces and x-ing outs. But he never stopped.

And eventually one day he got very sick, and soon thereafter he died, and soon after that he stopped typing. The bone-and-gristle Smith-Corona, his deformed twin, kept on typing for a few slow minutes after he passed, its keystrokes more labored and painful, until it ejected its last page, which read: He typed a lot, he really did, that's all he did, and now he's dead.

And eventually society overpowered his estate and the wishes of his family, and discovered the lost crypt of his secret writing, in a dry corner of a self-storage outfit in Tempe, Arizona, on a hundred-year lease. They clipped the lock and pried open the door and there inside the vault they found it, the novel, the life story of a man exactly like he had been, in every detail, except that he had not been born typing. 👁

More Wine?

More wine? No, I couldn't, well, yes, all right.
Fabulous. This is fabulous. You tell me that these
vegetables grow in the ground? They just pop up?
And you heat them in that pan and then ... this?
Impossible! Fabulous! Such a world! And this is the
sunrise? Every day you have this? What do you do
when the sun doesn't rise? Not once? That's a pretty
good record ... what do you call this? Ah! Delicious! I
am amazed. No, really, you are too kind. Now we are
going to see a movie, now we are riding our bicycles,
now we are talking on the telephone. Fabulous! I have
done nothing to deserve this world, it's so incredible! I
know there are places where nobody has anything but
rags, rags and ash and dirt. How am I so lucky? Well,
okay, but just one. Mmm! And a cherry inside?

Now we are racing our motorcycles. Now we are lying
in an open field, the only ones for miles around, you
my love and I. Rain falls straight up our noses. Clean
rain! It's a miracle! We roll and roll in the wheat and
weeds. Everywhere there is food and everything is
alive, and you are impossibly beautiful. Why me?
Why not one of them? I'm no saint. I'm not wealthy
in fat American dollars. Why is it that we are all so
happy? No, please, no more tiramisu, I'm sure I'll
explode.

My friends. There are so many of you. I hope I've
done enough to keep you happy and warm and alive. I
feel so powerless to help. Who have I made happy
who wasn't secretly happy already? What have I
changed? You are all so forgiving.

This life is exquisite. There is nobody I could be, no place I could live, and be happier than I am now. It's absurd! There's no reason, but I love you all so much. I'm a termite in a post, a nursing pig. I am drowning in my own pleasure. I'm laughing, I'm crying, I'm laughing. Why have you given me this? I don't deserve it. Thank you. Thank you! THANK YOU.

I promise I will love this world, and cherish it, and stand by it until my dying day, so help me life. ◈

I WAS AN ASSHOLE:
Afterword to the New Edition

In 1999 I attempted career suicide: I published myself.

Only the crappiest writers publish their own work.
They do it because no one else will have them, because
they write crap. At least, that is the widely reverberated
wisdom: publishing your own book is like tattooing
I SUCK DONKEY BALLS across your own forehead.
If you are fool enough to do this to yourself,
discriminating readers will discriminate against you,
critics will chortle, and publishing professionals will
refuse their delicious congress. You will die broke and
obscure, and if you're lucky enough to have a
tombstone it will read: HE SUCKED ACTUAL
DONKEY BALLS.

I knew that might happen — it may still — but I did
it anyway, out of desperation and spite, as a salve for a
lingering burning sensation in my soul left behind by a
totally mismanaged brush with Serious Literature.
Now, ten years later, as my oeuvre has continued its
stubborn growth and the pain in my heart has receded
to sub-bursitus levels, I am re-issuing this book — for
technical reasons that I'll explain — and taking the
occasion to re-examine the circumstances that drove
me to do it in the first place. Here's what happened:

It was spring of 1999, my future wife was pregnant
with our future child, and we were inspecting our
future home for any defects that might later lead to
marital collapse. That's why I was in the basement
with my head shoved through a tiny, filthy metal hatch
in the root of the central chimney, peering upward at a

distant postage stamp of blue sky framed by sketchy brickwork, trying to imagine what a fatally flawed chimney might look like, while my realtor and the homeowner chatted amicably about how to avoid the required permits for things, when Dave Eggers called me on my cell phone.

I had only just gotten a cell phone. They were newish to non-stockbrokers in 1999, and I had not yet developed a good sense of when to ignore the thing. Every conversation was full of novelty and amusement, still: "Hey, guess where I am? I'm driving! I'm at a movie! I'm in a chimney!" Maybe I should have let it go to voicemail, but instead I answered it, cramming my right hand through the hatch to wedge my brand new phone between a sooty brick wall and my head.

"This is Dave Eggers," said Dave Eggers. He sounded very far away; his voice was weirdly flat and emotionless, as if his cat had just died. (Chimney acoustics may have contributed to this.) He was calling about a story I'd sent to McSweeney's Quarterly Concern. He was thinking about running it in the second issue, because his people had liked it, and he wanted to know how I felt about that. He also wanted me to know that I spell my name funny, and did I really want to spell it that way, and would I mind if he made fun of that spelling in print?

How did I feel about that? A bunch of ways: thrilled, validated, tingly in my extremities, yet wary — why is he calling me up just to say "maybe"? — and

197

apprehensive, because I had only just forsaken an oath to never send my stories to magazines, because it had been such a drawn-out and disappointing torture when I was younger. The very first short story I ever sent out was published right away, but then for years I tried to publish my awful poetry and got nothing but boilerplate rejections from editors, or, worse, encouraging personal rejections from editors who wanted me to try again so they could reject me some more. And in all that time — a five-year initial effort out of high school to "become" a writer and "succeed" — I found many of the editors of these small poetry presses to be unpleasant little Napoleons who only valued other peoples' poetry as a decorative garnish around their own.

And who needed such jerks? Their cozy universe was being upended by a new, disrupting technology: a powerful communication medium that allowed anyone to broadcast their ideas at incredible speeds over long distances for almost no cost. It went unnoticed at first, but the shock waves from this new invention would eventually rattle the foundations of the publishing world, as it empowered a brave new generation of awful poets to emote more effusively than ever before.

This invention, of course, was the photocopier. My coworkers and I used to molest the one at work by squeezing our genitals against the glass, or chasing the glowing scanner with our teeth to make hideous paper masks of ourselves. Sometimes we would even copy our poems on the poor thing, amplifying their awfulness with the "enlarge" button, and then paste these up on the walls of our offices, or on the doors of the toilet stalls, or on telephone poles around town. Apparently the business cost of telling the employees to quit fucking around with the photocopier was greater than the cost of the photocopies themselves. That was the nineties in a nutshell: insufficient supervision.

So in exchange for access to the unknowable but likely tiny audiences of the small presses, I was quite content, for a while, to circulate little photocopied pamphlets among my friends and through the mail, and in return I received and read fantastically endearing 'zines such as COMETBUS and COOL BEANS and DORIS and others — many, many others, I have a basement full of others, you should stop by someday with a shovel ...

"Hello?" said Dave Eggers.

Sorry, right, here I am, yes. I told Dave I felt great (or awesome, or something like that) about that. It seemed like the correct answer. As for making fun of my name, I said Sure I Guess, although truly I was a bit offended; I actually consider that to be the very lowest form of humor. You will never be able to tell anybody a joke about their name that they haven't heard a million times already — a truth I'd expect someone named Eggers to know from experience.

But still, this had to be good, right? My story was accepted — well, no, it was maybe'd — by this pretty interesting and nicely designed literary magazine that seemed to have a wide distribution. It was only the second story I'd sent out since I broke my vow — the first came back from The Baffler with an encouraging note along the lines of "send us non-fiction" — so maybe I wasn't the only person who thought these stories of mine were any good. Perhaps my belief in myself was not wholly unfounded. And Dave Eggers — former editor of Might Magazine, though not yet the massive literary industry he was to become, but still a guy whose work I admired — had called me up to be weird and distant on the phone, and make fun of my name, and say maybe. I think I was supposed to be encouraged by that.

Instead it left me anxious, as did almost everything that spring and summer and fall, as my girlfriend and I bought that house, as we moved in and pulled up the carpet and painted the walls, as her belly ripened like an orange and we got married in front of a judge and signed our lives away to a bank. Everything was changing, everything was exciting and scary. Life was beginning, life was about to end. I hardly told anyone about the McSweeney's thing because, after all, he only said maybe.

Maybe a month later, as I was packing my extensive collection of heavy useless objects into cardboard boxes so I could throw them away after we moved, Dave Eggers called again. And it was just as awkward: mumbling, long pauses, occasional deep sighs. But this time he was "pretty sure" that my story had been accepted, pending some edits. He was going to e-mail me his notes; he said I could "take it or leave it" regarding those, and then send a draft back. I said Sure, Great, Yes, Awesome, words to that effect. He sounded disappointed.

But this, this was good, right? Could I brag to friends yet? "Pretty sure" seemed promising. But in retrospect I think it was the phrase "take it or leave it" that would derail my subway to stardom. Because I took that to mean I could look at his suggestions, consider each individually, and either take or leave it as I saw fit.

It takes two to miscommunicate, and I did my part. I received his editor's notes via e-mail, INSERTED IN ALL CAPS directly in the text so as to convey a strong YELLING AT YOU effect. And it's funny: I just dug out that list of notes today and read it again, and they are very minor edits, very reasonable, actually quite polite — very different from how I've remembered them over the last decade. I still don't agree with every last bit of it, but it's just little things here and there. Getting all worked up about it would have been pointlessly counter-productive.

But that's exactly what I did. At the time, those notes bugged the living shit out of me. I still don't get why. I could blame a typical writer's blend of ego and insecurity, or the general turbulence in my life at the time, or my lifelong issues with authority, or Dave's misunderstanding of the importance of the narrator's verbal tics to a vast novel-length story cycle that I planned to write but of course never did — the point is, I never did figure out how to trust Dave Eggers. I expected the worst. I assumed that at some point he would take away the candy and whip out the stick.

Believing this, I made it so, via a rapidly escalating exchange of defensive, grumpy e-mails over the course of an afternoon, bickering over shit like commas. By the end of the day, this big coup I had begun to believe in — bigger in retrospect, as McSweeney's went on to become The Next Big Thing in obscure literary magazines — had fallen apart and melted into a little lump of dog shit on the doorstep of my heart.

This is why I cannot have nice things: the Pulitzer Prize, the MacArthur Genius Grant, a blurb from Ted Nugent. Because, for all the difficult stuff I am good at, there were too many basic life skills I lacked at the adult age of thirty-two. Maybe still.

So down in flames plummeted the over-inflated zeppelin of my literary aspirations. And yet, I still had this giant pile of homeless stories in my lap. Some of these had appeared in a 'zine I put out irregularly called EYEHEART. Others I had distributed via a little mailing list, just to friends, just to get feedback I thought I could trust. Other stories weren't even stories, just strange little bits of text that had fallen out of my head, warm-up exercises or whatever, that I couldn't find it in me to crumple up and recycle. There was a huge stack of this stuff — more than two hundred individually-numbered bits of story, essay, poem, recipe, whatever — and I sought the advice of people I trusted, who told me I needed to publish these stories, somewhere, somehow.

So, having blocked the entrance to Literature for myself, and then having shat in the fire escape, I determined not to go down quietly. I whittled my stack down to about forty things and threw them together into one last 'zine, just to feel like all that time in front of the typing machines had amounted to something. A headstone, basically, for my dead career.

EYEHEART EVERYTHING is that 'zine. I printed it at Kinko's Copies in the middle of the night, just like all my other 'zines. The pages were cut by giant guillotine, and I stapled the spines and glued the covers myself. My brilliant friend Brady Clark did a fantastic job of the book design. It looked just like a Real Book — most people couldn't tell the difference. I put it on sale at Reading Frenzy, our local 'zine emporium that used to take consignment of anything with a staple in it. I gave free copies to friends, as always. I abandoned copies on the bus, snuck them into libraries, threw them at cops. I used a copy to steady a wobbly table leg. Any use was a good use.

Then a thing happened: the curator of the small-press section at Powell's City Of Books in Portland found a copy, liked it, asked for more. Suddenly I had a book featured prominently on the shelves of the largest bookstore on the West Coast. They have been re-ordering ever since.

The two printings of that first hand-bound edition of EYEHEART EVERYTHING add up to about seven hundred copies. And seven hundred sales, over a ten year period, means about as much to a major publisher as seven hundred squirrels farting in outer space. But to me, those sales are like seven hundred flaming pink candles on a bright orange birthday cake. This book opened doors for me everywhere. One copy was read by the CEO of a local entertainment firm and got me employment writing for film and television. Another copy was read by Carlton Mellick III; it begat a long a fruitful friendship and the eventual release of my first novel by Eraserhead Press. A short film was made from one of these stories, and several others were reprinted in various journals, online and off. I'm often asked to read from this book at literary events, or campfires, or weddings, and I always say yes. Best of all, some huge percentage of readers have bothered to track me down and tell me how much they loved this book. Had they not, I'm sure I would have succeeded in my furious effort to fail at writing.

Probably every headstrong young writer believes that they only need to find the audience who loves them for who they are, and that editors just get in the way. Probably every editor believes that writers are like uncut diamonds, in need of vigorous polishing and sharp blows with a chisel in order to realize their full potential. Probably the truth is somewhere in the middle. Looking back at this collection, I sure wish I'd had an editor. I see things I should have thrown away and things I should have sent to Granta or The New

Yorker — some of my best work, and some total crap, and nobody but myself in charge of knowing the difference. It was a snapshot taken at a poignant pivot point in my life. Ten years later, it's a historic document. Someday it might be valuable.

Many things happened to me in the intervening decade. We had that child. We bought that house. We got married a second time, in the backyard so everybody could watch. I did some journalism, some screen writing — I was once paid more than thirty thousand dollars to write fewer than ten lines of dialogue for a major motion picture — and I played a lot of music and wrote a lot of software and rode a lot of bicycles. Powell's continued to sell one or two or three copies of EYEHEART EVERYTHING every month, and I continued to manufacture more copies for them, ten or twenty at a time. I hot-glued the covers, and my daughter applied the little stickers with the ISBN barcodes — an absolutely crucial element of any professional book cover, by the way, and one that Brady and I forgot to include in the design, amateurs that we were.

Meanwhile, another thing happened entirely without me: Print On Demand. The publishing world has struggled for years now with how to love this bastard child of printing and the Internet, but I think it is the raddest thing ever. Basically, you can upload your book document digitally to a great big photocopier in the cloud, where robots hot-glue the covers so you don't have to. I positively would not have bothered printing my own book in the middle of the night at Kinko's, surrounded by muttering conspiracy theorists, sleepwalking office assistants and festive but foul-smelling methadrine addicts, if POD technology had existed in 1999.

(If I seem to harp on the hot glue, it's because I have suffered enough hot glue burns in the last ten years to cover most of my body. The seven hundredth book is finished and I'm not doing that any more. A hundred of something is a limited edition; seven hundred is a minimum wage.)

Today, POD technology is enabling droves of young, headstrong geniuses, who lack editors or even proofreaders, to publish their brilliant, flawless first novels without even lifting a stapler. This is both good and bad; some of these people really ought to wait. But who am I to tell them so? In the area of Not-Self-Publishing, I have zero credibility. It seems the printed word has simply broken free of parental supervision for the time being. That will be awesome and that will suck. My one piece of advice for the brave new wave of POD self-publishers is: don't forget the barcode.

This glossy new edition of EYEHEART EVERYTHING feels slightly bourgeois, but it's now distributed via major catalogs, it can be shipped overnight (if you're really that desperate), it's more correctly spelled than ever, has much finer registration and no longer triggers airport metal detectors. Also, the story "UHF" now includes most of Dave Eggers' suggested improvements. I love to make beautiful things, and I truly believe that the POD edition of EYEHEART EVERYTHING is the loveliest thing POD can produce. Plus, it remains an excellent tool for stabilizing a wobbly table.

But you may have to take my word for that; you may in fact be reading these words on a digital e-book reader, or a super-intelligent telephone, or a beam of pink light that implants short stories and medical advice directly in your brain. The future will be full of crazy stuff like that! I would never discriminate against your preferred book-input port. Please just know that there was once a time when people made books with their hands, out of paper and ink, and handed them directly to one another, and read them with their eyes, and held them to their hearts. It was sweet.

- mykle hansen - September 15, 2010 -